W9-DFJ-655

replica

Rewind
The Plague Trilogy
Book I

MARILYN KAYE

BANTAM BOOKS
NEW YORK • TORONTO • LONDON • SYDNEY • AUCKLAND

RL 5.5, 008–012

REWIND

A Bantam Skylark Book / February 2002

All rights reserved.
Copyright © 2002 by Marilyn Kaye
Cover art copyright© 2002 by Craig White

No part of this book may be reproduced or transmitted in any form or by any
means, electronic or mechanical, including photocopying, recording, or by
any information storage and retrieval system, without permission in writing
from the publisher. For information address Bantam Books.

If you purchased this book without a cover you should be aware that this book
is stolen property. It was reported as "unsold and destroyed" to the publisher
and neither the author nor the publisher has received any payment for this
"stripped book."

ISBN: 0-553-48763-9

Visit us on the Web! www.randomhouse.com/kids
Educators and librarians, for a variety of teaching tools, visit us at
www.randomhouse.com/teachers

Published simultaneously in the United States and Canada

Bantam Skylark is an imprint of Random House Children's Books, a division of
Random House, Inc. SKYLARK BOOK and colophon and BANTAM BOOKS
and colophon are registered trademarks of Random House, Inc. Bantam Books,
1540 Broadway, New York, New York 10036.

PRINTED IN THE UNITED STATES OF AMERICA

OPM   10 9 8 7 6 5 4 3 2 1

For Marie-Emmanuele Amphoux

Rewind

 one

In the Parkside Middle School media center, Amy kept her voice low as she read aloud from the encyclopedia.

" 'No one knows exactly why the dinosaurs disappeared completely from the face of the earth, but evidence indicates that dinosaurs died out approximately sixty-five million years ago.' " She looked up. "Did you get that, Linda? Sixty-five million years ago."

Linda turned the page of her *Seventeen*.

"Linda?" Amy realized the girl couldn't hear her. The flaps on her weird headgear had slipped down and were completely covering her ears. Amy leaned across the table and poked her.

Linda jumped and shrieked. This caused practically every student in the media center to do the same. The librarian, Ms. Marino, glared at them all.

Amy pointed to the flaps over Linda's ears, and Linda lifted them.

"Don't scare me like that!" she said.

"Sorry." Amy couldn't blame her for overreacting. Everyone was jumpy these days. "I was just telling you that dinosaurs disappeared sixty-five million years ago."

"Okay," Linda said.

"Write it down," Amy insisted.

Linda obliged. Amy leaned over the table to watch. Muffling a sigh of exasperation, she added three zeros to the number Linda had written. "Sixty-five *million*, Linda. Not thousand."

"Yeah, whatever." Linda returned to her magazine.

Amy leaned back in her chair and mentally harangued the social studies teacher who had assigned the partners for this project. Could Amy possibly have been given a worse partner than Linda Riviera? Was there a lazier person in the entire eighth grade at Parkside Middle School? From the second the teacher had announced the partners in class, Amy had known she would end up doing all the work.

Of course, it wasn't going to be all that difficult for her, not with her special abilities. She could read faster, absorb information more quickly, and whip up a decent report more easily than anyone in the class. Still, it wasn't fair that Linda would reap the rewards of Amy's superior intelligence.

She went back to the encyclopedia article. " 'The first humanlike beings appeared on earth about three point six million years ago,' " she reported. But those flaps on Linda's helmet had fallen back over her ears, and she didn't hear. Amy risked another little poke. At least this time Linda didn't scream.

"Could you *please* take that stupid thing off your head?" Amy begged.

"Are you crazy?" Linda snapped. "My father spent a fortune on this helmet. It's the best protection money can buy. Maybe *you* don't care if you drop dead, but *I* do."

"I care," Amy muttered.

"But you're not even wearing a mask," Linda pointed out.

Amy looked around at the other students in the media center. Some were working quietly in small groups, others were reading, a few were at the computer terminals. Almost all of them wore surgical masks covering their nose and mouth.

"My mother says those masks can't protect anyone from the Plague," Amy told her.

"How does *she* know?"

"She just happens to be a scientist. And she told me whatever this disease is, it's not a virus. It's not like the cold or the flu. You can't catch it from being around someone who's coughing or sneezing."

Linda didn't buy this. "I heard on the news that nobody knows what causes the Plague."

"Yeah, that's true. But they know it's not contagious."

Linda shrugged. "Well, *I'm* not taking any chances."

Amy knew it wasn't worth getting into an argument. Lots of people felt the way Linda did. Even though all the news reports told the public the disease didn't appear to be contagious, people were wearing masks and looking suspiciously over their shoulder at the slightest sound of a cough or a sneeze. No one believed that coughs and sneezes weren't symptoms of this particular terrible illness.

But Amy couldn't blame people for not being logical. They were scared. The whole world was scared.

It seemed to come out of nowhere, this disease. The first few cases had popped up on a different continent, making it a distant, spooky, vague threat. Then the cases had multiplied and spread to other continents—

including North America. Articles had appeared in the science sections of magazines, and now on the covers of *Time* and *Newsweek*.

The disease remained a mystery—and it was spreading more quickly. Just last week, headlines in local newspapers declared that three cases had been diagnosed right here in Los Angeles. One of the victims had already died. Another was in what they called a permanent vegetative state, which didn't sound very pleasant. The third had recovered—sort of. But he was now in a wheelchair. Doctors had given the disease a long, unpronounceable scientific name, but everyone else just called it the Plague. With a capital *P*.

The symptoms varied: Some people started feeling tired, others became anxious. Some had headaches, some had backaches. In some victims, the disease progressed slowly. Others fell apart overnight. Ultimately, they all collapsed and went into a coma. Some people came out of the comas but suffered severe brain damage. Blindness, deafness, and paralysis were common. Some people lost their memory. Others went completely insane. The majority didn't survive.

All kinds of medical researchers were examining the stricken patients, running tests, studying blood samples under microscopes. They could see that something was clearly wrong. Actually, that wasn't exactly it. They could see that something was wrong—but there was nothing clear about it. Where had the Plague come from? How had people caught it? No one could figure it out. And tension, anxiety, and depression hovered over the earth like a fog.

At Parkside Middle School, as everywhere else in the world, the fear was present. But teachers and parents were determined to try to keep life as normal as possible for the students. So the kids went to classes, ate their lunches, did their homework assignments, and challenged the occasional school regulation. In fact, at that very moment in the school media center, a major rule was being broken. Someone had left a cell phone on, and it was ringing.

Ms. Marino's head jerked up sharply again. Half the students in the media center frantically rummaged through their backpacks and handbags. Amy checked her own cell phone to make sure it was turned off. Not that she used it much. Her best friend, Tasha, didn't have a cell phone, and Amy's mother knew better than to call her at school.

The earflaps didn't prevent Linda from hearing and identifying the ring. She dove into her bag and pulled out a phone.

"Hello? Hi! No, really? What did he say?"

Linda was so engrossed in her conversation, she didn't even notice Ms. Marino glaring at her. Two seconds later, the librarian was standing by their table.

"What's going on here, young lady? You know the rules about cell phones!"

"I gotta go," Linda said hastily, and clicked the Off button. The librarian gave a stern "don't let me catch you on that phone again" look and returned to her desk.

"Linda, come on, let's work," Amy urged.

Linda sighed. "What's the point?"

"The point is that this report is due in two weeks."

Linda sighed again. "If we're *alive* in two weeks." Her eyes filled with tears.

Amy had no response. She was determined to think positively. Her mother had assured her that public panic was spreading faster than the Plague itself, and that every hospital and laboratory in the world was working on finding the cause—and a cure. Her mother's friend Dr. Dave Hopkins was one of a team of doctors working on the Plague, and he believed they were on the verge of making an important discovery.

Amy was lost in thought when she saw Tasha in the media center's entrance. She looked agitated. Amy waved to her, and Tasha came over to the table where Amy and Linda were working.

"Have you guys seen Simone Cusack?" Tasha wanted

to know. "She's supposed to meet me here so we can work on the social studies project."

"I think she's absent," Amy said. "She wasn't in homeroom." She turned to another student at the end of their table. "Layne, have you seen Simone around?"

"I think she's sick," Layne said. "She called me last night and said she wasn't feeling good."

Linda gasped. "Ohmigod, Simone's sick?"

Amy knew what she was thinking. "Linda, there are a lot of sicknesses in the world. She could have a cold, or the flu. Or chicken pox, for crying out loud."

"Or something a lot worse," Linda said darkly. "Hey, Jason," she called out to a passing student.

The boy turned. "What?"

"You know Simone Cusack? She's *sick*." Linda emphasized the word and gave the boy a meaningful look. Jason got the message. He drew in his breath sharply.

"You think it's . . ." Clearly, he couldn't even bring himself to say the word.

Amy glared at Linda in disgust. "Oh, for Pete's sake . . ." Linda was famous for her ability to get a rumor started faster than anyone else. This had to be stopped, immediately.

Amy looked toward the librarian's desk. Ms. Marino wasn't there. Quickly Amy whipped out her cell phone, turned it on, and hit some buttons.

"Who are you calling?" Tasha asked.

"Simone," Amy replied.

Linda looked at her curiously. "You know Simone's number by heart?"

Amy didn't bother to answer. She couldn't very well tell Linda that her memory was so sharp, she had the entire school directory in her head.

"Hello, Ms. Cusack? This is Amy Candler. I'm a friend of Simone's. Is Simone sick?" She listened to the woman's explanation, thanked her, and ended the call.

She turned to the others triumphantly. "Simone's in the hospital. She had her appendix taken out this morning. She's going to be absolutely fine."

Jason and Tasha breathed sighs of relief. So did Linda, even though she was probably disappointed that she couldn't report the first case of the Plague at Parkside.

"You want to know what I think?" Linda asked. No one did, but she told them anyway. "I think everyone who gets the Plague should be put on a deserted island in the middle of the ocean."

"Are you crazy?" Tasha asked. "They need to be in hospitals, with doctors and nurses!"

"Yeah," Jason agreed fervently. "They'd *all* die without treatment!"

"Besides," Amy piped up. "I told you, the Plague isn't

contagious. Quarantining the victims wouldn't do any good!" She was getting very irritated by Linda's attitude, and she could hear her voice rising.

Unfortunately, Ms. Marino had returned, and she could hear it too. As she strode toward them, she was looking seriously annoyed.

"How many times do I have to tell you people to keep the noise down?" she asked. The words had barely left her mouth when another cell phone started ringing. Now the librarian was furious.

"Whose phone is that?" she demanded.

Amy's stomach belly flopped. She'd forgotten to turn off her phone after calling Simone. "Mine," she said weakly. She grabbed it out of her bag and hit the Off button.

The ringing stopped, but that didn't make Ms. Marino any happier. She glared at Amy. "*You* have detention today, young lady."

Amy opened her mouth to protest. After all, Linda's phone had rung earlier, and *she* hadn't gotten detention. Amy was only being punished because this was the last straw for the librarian. It wasn't fair!

But she shut her mouth. There was no point in complaining. All she would hear was the response every adult gave when a kid complained that some particular punishment wasn't fair.

Life wasn't fair.

t w 2

Amy left school an hour later than usual, along with the rest of Parkside's delinquent element that had been kept after school for detention. She was embarrassed to find herself in the company of two notoriously bad kids and one boy who'd been caught cheating on a quiz.

The word would spread, and tomorrow she'd have to explain why she'd had to stay after school. If that wasn't enough to put her in a foul mood, she had the certainty of facing her mother's annoyance. Dr. Dave was coming over for dinner that night, and Amy had promised to straighten up the house before Nancy

Candler got home from work. She'd be home by now, she'd have seen the mess, and she'd be furious that Amy hadn't done as she'd promised.

Maybe Amy could ward off some of the fury as she walked home. She could offer to run an errand, pick up fresh bread for dinner, something like that. Pulling out her cell phone, she turned it on. But before she could punch #1 to connect her directly to her home number, she noticed a blinking sign on the screen.

It wasn't something she'd ever seen before, but she recognized it from the instruction book. It meant that she had missed a call. Of course—it was the call that had come through in the media center. She pressed another button and held the phone to her ear. There was no message, only a mechanical voice telling her the phone number the call had been made from. It wasn't familiar—probably a wrong number. Now she was even more annoyed. She'd had to suffer detention for someone else's stupid mistake.

Then she noticed another blinking signal. She had a text message. She hit a couple of buttons and watched the screen. In less than a second, the message appeared.

Friday. 9:00 P.M. Uncle Billy.

This made no sense whatsoever. Amy had no Uncle Billy—she had no uncles at all, or aunts either. But apparently, someone with a number similar to hers did have an Uncle Billy, and unless he realized his mistake, he'd be expecting someone at nine o'clock tonight who wouldn't show up. Well, too bad—Amy had enough problems of her own to worry about. Which reminded her to call her mother.

She hit #1. Nancy Candler picked up on the first ring. "Hello?"

"Mom, it's me." Amy gritted her teeth in anticipation of the explosion.

"Hi, honey. Is something wrong?"

"No, nothing's wrong." She waited for the natural question, "Then why are you so late getting home?"

It didn't come. Instead, her mother asked, "Why are you calling? Remember, we agreed that you wouldn't use the cell phone for chatting."

"Um, well, I was just calling to see if you wanted me to pick anything up on the way home. For dinner."

"Dinner?" Her mother sounded puzzled.

"Yeah. Dr. Dave's coming, right?"

She could hear the sharp intake of breath at the other end of the line. "Oh no. I completely forgot."

Amy rolled her eyes. Her mother was doing a lot of that lately—forgetting stuff. It had to be her age. After all, Nancy Candler was almost forty. "So do you want me to pick something up?"

"Honey, could you? I've got pasta and salad stuff.

Maybe you could stop at the bakery and get some fresh bread. And something for dessert. Oh, and I need a bottle of wine."

"Well, I can't get *that* for you," Amy said.

"Why not?"

"Mom! I'm underage! They don't sell wine to minors!"

There was a moment of silence, and then her mother laughed. "Of course, I know that. What's the matter with me? I must be losing my mind. Just pick up the bread and dessert, honey, and I'll be eternally grateful."

"Okay, Mom." Amy couldn't believe her good fortune. No mention whatsoever of the mess at home or the fact that she was late leaving school. Maybe her luck for the day was turning.

She picked up the bread and a pie and arrived home to find her mother in the dining room, setting the table. That was usually Amy's job, but her mother just continued to roll the cloth napkins and place them in rings.

"Want some help?" Amy offered.

"No thanks, honey. Everything's under control."

Nancy looked tired, though. Amy made a mental note to clear the table and put the dishes in the dishwasher immediately after dinner, without even waiting to be asked.

Meanwhile, it appeared that her luck was holding—and with that in mind, she ran up to her room to check her e-mail. Maybe there would be a message from Andy and Chris.

Ever since the two boys had taken off together a couple of months earlier, she'd heard from one or the other, sometimes both of them, at least once a week. Andy was a clone, like Amy. He and his "brothers" had been created during the first part of Project Crescent, conducted two years before the Amys were made. Andy had recently discovered that his adoptive father was in league with the organization, the group that had funded Project Crescent and still hoped to pull the clones together to start a master race. Feeling betrayed, Andy had left home.

Chris was a clone too—but unlike Amy and Andy, he wasn't genetically designed. He'd been cloned from a man who wanted spare parts available, just in case one of his own organs broke down. Leaving his so-called father, Chris had been placed in foster care—only to learn that his foster parents were also connected to the organization, and had only taken him in to get closer to Amy.

Homeless and parentless, the boys had joined together and gone off in search of the organization.

They sent Amy messages from Internet cafés whenever they had a chance. But she hadn't heard from them in two weeks, and she was getting a little worried.

Logging on, Amy went directly to her e-mail. There was only one item, and it wasn't from the boys. She didn't know *who* had sent it—it was listed as coming from an Unknown Sender. The message was brief.

Friday. 9:00 P.M. Uncle Billy.

Now this was getting weird. Maybe Uncle Billy was a code name, something Andy and Chris had dreamed up to use when they contacted her, just in case the organization was tracing e-mails. Maybe they were telling Amy to meet them tonight. But why Uncle Billy? And where was she supposed to meet them?

"Amy!"

She left her room and looked down at her mother, who stood at the bottom of the stairs. "What's up, Mom?"

"I'm going out to pick up some ice cream for dessert. I'll be right back."

"Mom! I brought an apple pie home for dessert, remember? I showed it to you ten minutes ago!" She started down the stairs. "Mom, do you feel okay? You're acting weird."

"I'm fine," Nancy assured her, but her voice was

tired. "Just wiped out, I guess. Well, I'm glad I don't have to go out for ice cream."

At that moment, something clicked in Amy's head. Ice cream—Uncle Billy's Ice Cream Shop! It was a small café just a mile away, in a strip mall. That was where she was supposed to meet her friends.

A tremor of excitement tickled her spine. Something was going on, and the fact that the boys were being so mysterious about contacting her meant it could be something big. She was glad Dr. Dave was coming for dinner. His presence would keep her mother occupied.

During the dinner, however, Nancy didn't show much interest in anything. She was polite. She smiled and nodded as Dr. Dave and Amy talked, but she didn't really take part in the conversation. Dr. Dave didn't notice anything unusual, though. He was too excited, talking about new developments in the Plague research.

"It looks like we've come up with a reliable test for the disease," he told them. "It's a simple skin patch. If someone's carrying the Plague, they'll have a reaction in twenty-four hours."

"What kind of reaction?" Amy asked him.

"A pink rash. It's a clear indication, and it can pinpoint the disease at an early stage, even before the victim shows any symptoms. Early diagnosis can be very helpful."

"How?" Amy asked. "There's still no cure, is there?"

"No, I'm afraid not. Until we know what's causing the Plague, I doubt we'll be able to find a cure. All we've been able to do so far is rule things out. We know the disease isn't caused by anything we're eating or drinking. It's not in the air."

Nancy roused herself enough to ask, "Could it be some kind of biological warfare?"

"No, that doesn't make any sense," Dr. Dave replied. "The disease isn't directed at any one group or country. It's hitting people everywhere, it's completely random. At least with the patch, we can make an early diagnosis. Complete bed rest seems to slow down the progress of the disease. And the longer we can keep people alive, the better chance they seem to have of— of some recovery."

Amy knew why he'd hesitated just then. From what she'd heard and read, hardly anyone made a complete recovery. Even if they didn't die, they suffered some kind of damage.

Dr. Dave continued to talk about the patch, about the chemicals and natural ingredients that were absorbed into the skin. He was mainly talking to Nancy, since as a scientist, she would understand more than

Amy could. Amy was able to take surreptitious glances at her watch and think about what kind of excuse she could use to get out of the house. She cleared the table and put the dishes in the dishwasher. When she returned to the table, Dr. Dave was still talking about the patch.

"Excuse me, Dr. Dave. Mom, can I go over to Tasha's? We're working on a project."

"What?" Nancy looked at her vaguely. "Oh, sure."

That was easy, Amy thought. But when she left the house, she noticed her mother standing at the window. Nancy didn't actually seem to be watching Amy, but Amy couldn't take any chances. She'd have to make a brief stop at Tasha's.

Tasha opened the door. "Hi! Come on in."

Amy followed her inside, where Eric was sprawled in front of the TV. He gave Amy a salute. "What's up?"

"I got a message from Andy and Chris. They're in town." She told them about the text message on her phone and the identical e-mail note.

"How can you be sure the messages were from the boys?" Tasha wanted to know.

"I'm not," Amy admitted. "But who else could it be?"

That was a dumb thing to ask. Considering some of the characters she'd encountered in the past, she wasn't surprised when Eric declared he'd be going with her.

And of course, Tasha wasn't about to be left behind. The Morgans' parents weren't home, so they didn't need to make up an excuse. And when they left the house, Nancy Candler was no longer at the window.

Amy wasn't sorry to have the company of her friends. What had seemed exciting earlier had become a little scary in the dark of night. As they made their way to Uncle Billy's, they considered the purpose of the meeting.

"I thought Chris and Andy were going to Washington, D.C.," Tasha said. "Why are they back in Los Angeles?"

"Maybe the organization is doing something here," Amy suggested.

"Yeah," Eric said. "Like, maybe they're all tossing back milkshakes at Uncle Billy's right now. You know, those messages could be a trick to get you there, Amy."

"I know," Amy said. "Which is why I'm glad you guys are with me." She tried to sound convincingly confident. Even so, in the back of her mind, she wondered how Eric and Tasha would deal with the possibility that kidnappers were waiting for them at Uncle Billy's.

But she felt better as they approached the café. Brightly lit, it was full of customers. Happy-looking people sat at little round tables, digging into bowls or licking cones. Waiters in red-and-white uniforms were buzzing around, and lively music was playing in the background. It didn't look like the kind of place where anything bad could happen.

Even so, Amy and her friends entered cautiously. They stood just inside the doorway and scoped the place. Tasha grabbed Amy's arm.

"Over there, by the sorbet," she hissed. "The guy with the sunglasses, in the leather jacket. Is that Chris?"

Amy shook her head. "He's too tall." She had her eyes on another boy, whose back was to them. Would Andy have dyed his hair black? Then the boy turned toward them. And unless Andy had not only dyed his hair but had also undergone major plastic surgery, it wasn't him.

"I don't see either of them," Eric said.

"Maybe they're late," Amy said. "Why don't we sit down at a table and wait a while?" She indicated an empty table in the back. "We can watch the door from there."

"Can we get some ice cream while we're waiting?" Tasha asked hopefully.

"Sure, why not?" Amy couldn't resist taking a look at what other people were having as she passed their tables. The rocky road looked particularly good. But Uncle Billy's also had some really interesting exotic

flavors, and she was tempted by the caramel macadamia nut chocolate chip. How was she going to
choose? And how could anyone come into a place like
this and only order coffee? Like that man over there,
sitting alone . . .

As if he could read her mind, the man looked up as
they passed him. His face was clearly visible to her.
And Amy gasped.

Tasha and Eric both stopped in their tracks.

"Amy? What's wrong?" Tasha asked anxiously.

"Do you see them?" Eric asked.

Momentarily unable to speak, Amy could only shake
her head. There was no sign of Andy or Chris in the
café. But she was looking directly into the eyes of
someone else she recognized very well.

She found her voice, but she could only speak in a
whisper.

"Mr. Devon . . ."

th3ee

When was the last time she had seen the mysterious man who came in and out of her life? Months before, on a beautiful island in the middle of nowhere. She couldn't even be sure if this person was the real Mr. Devon, the man she'd first known as the assistant principal of her middle school. On a lonely highway up north, she'd seen him slumped over the steering wheel of a car—dead. Or maybe not. Because on the paradise island, she'd seen many other Mr. Devons.

His dark eyes bored into hers. There was no way she could know if this was the original Mr. Devon or any of the other Devons she'd encountered so far in her life, in so many different places and situations. Even as he watched her, she could see no sign of recognition on his face.

Knowing her own expression showed shock and disbelief, she took a deep breath and tried to stay calm. She made her way closer to him. "Hello. I think you're expecting me."

He gave a curt nod. "*Only* you."

She remembered that Eric and Tasha were standing on either side of her. They were both gaping at Mr. Devon. They'd seen him before, and they didn't know how to react to the sight of him. Like Amy, they knew he was a puzzle. Like Amy, they didn't know whose side he was on.

Mr. Devon had lured Amy into dangerous predicaments. He'd also saved her life. According to Andy, he wasn't to be trusted. But her own mother had paid heed to his advice on several occasions. He'd been seen conspiring with the organization. But when the organization came too close, he'd arranged Amy's escape. He seemed to know everything, but he told nothing. Was he friend or foe? Good or evil?

Right now, the expression on his face wasn't exactly friendly. Amy tried not to feel intimidated. "These are my friends," she told him. "Eric and Tasha Morgan."

"I know," he said.

Well, *that's* interesting, she thought. He might be the original Devon, then, the one who'd worked at Parkside. Or maybe all the Devons had the same memories.

"Then you know that they can be trusted," Amy said. "Whatever you want to tell me, you can tell them too."

He continued to look at them, unblinking and without expression. He didn't say anything, but he didn't have to. Amy knew he wasn't about to talk to her in the presence of her friends.

In the past, she'd always caved in to Mr. Devon. She'd always assumed that he knew more and that he knew better than she did. But this time, she rebelled. She'd been through dangerous experiences on her own; she'd saved herself without his help. And if Andy was right, she shouldn't trust Devon any more than Devon wanted to trust her friends.

She met his stern gaze without flinching. "I'm willing to listen," she said. "But only if you let them listen too."

Finally, he gave her an almost imperceptible nod. He was sitting at a table for two, and there was only one other chair. Amy and her friends moved to a recently vacated booth. Mr. Devon joined them there.

A red-and-white-uniformed waiter appeared by their side. "Hi, folks, what can I get you?"

25

Mr. Devon shook his head, indicating that he already had his coffee, and made a gesture that dismissed the waiter. But Amy was still feeling assertive, and she didn't want Devon thinking she could be pushed around.

"One scoop of rocky road and one scoop of macadamia nut," she told the waiter.

"You want nuts on that?" he asked.

"Okay," she said.

"Whipped cream?"

"Yes."

"Sprinkles? M&M's? Reese's Pieces? Crushed Oreos?"

Amy pondered the choices. That was when she noticed how the usually impassive Mr. Devon was actually showing a flash of irritation in his eyes. "Uh, Oreos, please," she said.

Tasha and Eric ordered more quickly. As soon as the waiter left the table, Mr. Devon began to speak. He ignored Tasha and Eric and talked to Amy as if they were alone at the table.

"I need a sample of your bone marrow," he said bluntly.

Amy blinked. "Huh?"

He repeated the statement. "I've made arrangements for you at a local hospital. It's a simple procedure, nothing for you to worry about. You can lose a certain amount of bone marrow without suffering any consequences."

"I *know* that," Amy informed him. "What I want to know is why you want *mine*."

He hesitated. "It would be best if you could simply trust me on this. The less you know, the better off you are."

"Maybe so," Amy said. "But I still want to know more."

He glanced at Tasha and Eric, then spoke to Amy. "The information is highly confidential."

"If you want me to trust you, you're going to have to trust my friends," Amy replied.

He studied her for a moment. "You may be putting your friends in danger."

Eric spoke. "We'll take that risk."

"Yes," Tasha agreed.

This time, it seemed to Amy that Mr. Devon glanced at her friends with something like respect. And he gave in.

"I'll come right to the point. You know about the Plague." He phrased that as a statement, not a question, but they all nodded in response. "We've come onto some important information regarding the disease."

Amy wanted to ask him who he meant by *we*, but she held her tongue. There were some things she had a feeling she would never know.

"We now know that the so-called Plague is the result of genetic residue," he continued. "Millions of years ago, early humans encountered some unusual bacteria. No one knows the source of these bacteria. There's no evidence that it came from anything natural that's still on the planet. But we do know that these bacteria caused the mutation of a gene, which resulted in this disease."

"Wait a minute," Amy interjected. "Are you saying the Plague is a genetic disorder? If that's true, how come we're just hearing about it now? Wouldn't all the descendants of those early humans be carrying the gene?"

"That would be a logical assumption," Mr. Devon said. "However, in this case, the gene lay dormant and ultimately deteriorated to the point where it had no impact on the human body. Then, just recently, there's been a sort of spontaneous mutation. The residue is reforming, it's regenerating. We don't know why—it could have something to do with ecology and changes in the environment. What we do know is that the newly mutated gene is producing that original bacteria."

"And that's the Plague," Amy said.

Mr. Devon nodded.

Tasha looked hopeful. "That's good news, isn't it? I read in an article that finding the source is the first step to finding a cure."

"That's true," Mr. Devon admitted. "Now we have to figure out how to stop the gene from mutating."

Now Amy understood. "That's why you want my bone marrow. Because my genes are perfect and won't mutate."

"Yes. Genetically designed clones seem to have a natural immunity. A sample of clone bone marrow may provide scientists with the information needed to create an antidote. And maybe even a vaccine to prevent future cases."

Slowly, Amy nodded. "That makes sense. Okay, what do I have to do?"

"Hold on," Eric broke in. "How come you're only asking Amy for bone marrow? What about all the other clones?"

Mr. Devon sighed. "Unfortunately, as Amy could tell you, many of the other Amys aren't the kind of people who want to save humanity. Those who are, we haven't been able to locate. We'll continue to look, of course, but in the meantime . . ."

"It's okay, Eric," Amy said. "I don't mind giving bone marrow if there's a chance it can stop the Plague."

"Good," Mr. Devon said. "I'll give you the address of the clinic, and—"

"Excuse me," Tasha said suddenly. "I'm going to the rest room."

Mr. Devon rolled his eyes. "And I'll meet you at the clinic, Amy. At two o'clock."

"Amy, come with me," Tasha demanded.

Amy looked at her in surprise.

"Why do girls always have to go to the rest room in pairs?" Eric wondered.

Amy was wondering the same thing, mainly because Tasha wasn't the kind of girl who did that. But under the table, she felt Tasha's kick. There had to be a reason.

"Okay. Excuse me, Mr. Devon, I'll be right back."

The minute they stepped into the rest room, Tasha checked under the stalls to make sure they were alone. Then she got right to the point.

"Are you *crazy*?"

"Giving bone marrow isn't that big a deal," Amy told her. "Chris did it, remember? I'll be fine."

Tasha rolled her eyes. "For someone who's super-smart, you're not thinking. Amy, a sample of your bone marrow contains a lot of information. Your DNA, for example. Giving bone marrow is like handing over a recipe for making more clones like you. If that bone marrow got into the wrong hands, can you imagine the consequences?"

"Mr. Devon wouldn't let that happen," Amy said. But even as she said the words, she was having second thoughts. Why was she suddenly so sure he was on the level? He'd always had a way of making her believe him. Just minutes before, she had been remembering how mysterious Mr. Devon was, how she never really knew if he was a friend or an enemy. She'd wondered if he was working with the organization. And now here she was, ready to hand over the blueprint to her entire being!

But on the other hand, could she say no? What if her bone marrow really could save people?

"I need to think about this," she said finally.

"Exactly," Tasha agreed.

Mr. Devon wasn't pleased to hear that she'd changed her mind.

"I need time," Amy told him. "I need time to process everything."

"Amy, we don't have time," he said testily.

But Amy was adamant. "I need time. And you keep saying *we*. Who's *we*? I want some details. You can't just pop into my life and expect me to turn over some bone marrow. I need to know more."

"I can't tell you more," he said. But he took a pen and jotted something down on a napkin. "You can reach me at this number." He handed her the napkin and walked out of the café.

"Geez, he didn't even say goodbye," Tasha said.

"And I guess he's not going to pay for the ice cream," Eric added. But they enjoyed their treats anyway. And Amy decided to put off thinking about Mr. Devon's request until the next day.

It was late when they returned to their condo community, but Amy was surprised to see that no lights were on in her house. She knew her mother must have gone to bed early, but normally Nancy would have left a light on for her. Saying goodbye to Tasha and Eric, Amy put her key in the lock.

Inside, she decided not to turn on a lamp—her mother was a light sleeper, and Amy didn't want to wake her. Her good intentions didn't pan out. Moving around in the darkness, she knocked over a vase. It hit the floor with a crash.

Amy froze, waiting for her mother's voice. It didn't come. She put a light on and went into the kitchen to get a broom to sweep up the glass shards. In the kitchen, she saw a note stuck with a magnet on the refrigerator door.

That was when she learned why the smashed vase hadn't woken her mother. Nancy Candler wasn't home. Dr. Dave had written the note.

Amy—
Your mother became sick, and I've taken her to the hospital. Call me.
Dr. Dave

With a shaking hand, Amy punched in the digits of Dr. Dave's cell phone number. He answered immediately.

"What happened?" Amy asked frantically. "Is Mom okay?"

"She fainted after dinner," Dr. Dave told her.

"But what's wrong with her?" Amy asked. "Is it the flu? Maybe she was just exhausted."

There was a moment of hesitation before Dr. Dave spoke carefully. "We don't know what's wrong, Amy. We're going to run some tests."

Something about his voice sent a chill through her. Suddenly, she couldn't breathe. "Dr. Dave, do you think it could be . . ." She couldn't bring herself to say the words. But he knew what she was asking.

"We just don't know, Amy."

fur

Amy burst through the swinging doors of the hospital emergency room. She was slightly out of breath. She'd run all the way from home, which wasn't easy, even for someone in her perfect physical condition. A man in a white coat looked at her with concern.

"What's wrong?" he asked.

"My mother," Amy said breathlessly. "I have to find her. She's here in the hospital, and—"

But the doctor or nurse or whoever he was became distracted by the arrival of paramedics pushing one stretcher after another through swinging doors.

"Multiple-car pileup on the interstate," someone was yelling, and all the uniformed people converged on the stretchers.

Amy followed the man she'd spoken to. "My mother, do you know where she is? Nancy Candler."

The man responded in a rush. "Wait in chairs," he ordered.

She couldn't blame him for pushing her aside. The people on the stretchers looked as if they were in pretty bad shape. She saw what he meant by *Wait in chairs*. There was a big waiting room, where people in various states of unhappiness were sitting. She couldn't tell which ones were waiting for treatment and which ones were waiting for family and friends. Everyone looked miserable. And they all seemed as if they'd been waiting there a long, long time.

This was why Dr. Dave had told her not to come. He'd said there was nothing she could do, and she wouldn't even be allowed to see her mother. Nancy was being quarantined until all the medical tests were completed. And even if Amy could somehow find the room where her mother was being treated, it wouldn't help much. Dr. Dave had said Nancy was unconscious—and would probably remain in that condition for a while.

But there was no way Amy could just stay home and wait. And she couldn't just sit here and wait either. Purposefully, she headed toward the nurses' station.

"Excuse me, I have to find—"

"Wait in chairs, please," the nurse recited as she pushed by to wheel a bleeding man into an examining room.

She wasn't being unkind, and Amy understood the situation. With all these sick and wounded people around, no one was going to waste time on a girl in perfectly good health. She found a semiquiet corner and pulled out her cell phone.

Apparently, Dr. Dave was too busy to answer his phone. Impatiently, she waited for the beep so she could leave a message. "It's me, Amy, I'm here at the hospital, in the emergency room. Could you come find me?"

She paced the emergency room and tried to remember when she'd ever felt so frightened. Frightening situations were nothing new to her; both she and her mother had been in grave danger before. But somehow, this seemed worse. Every other time, Amy had been able to use her strength or her intellect to rescue her mother or save herself. If this was really and truly the Plague, there was absolutely nothing she could do.

All the strength and intellect in the world couldn't cure an incurable disease. And that was the scariest thing of all. To be completely helpless . . .

All around her there was pain. A woman held her head and grimaced, a man clutched his swollen wrist, a young child wailed. Amy wasn't the only person on the planet who was suffering. Her mother wasn't the only sick person in the world. But she found no comfort in knowing this.

When her cell phone rang, Amy practically dropped it in her rush to press the right button.

"Hello? Dr. Dave?"

But it wasn't Dr. Dave. For a second, Amy couldn't identify the tentative voice that asked, "Amy?" Then she heard "Amy, is that you?" and she knew who was on the line.

"Andy!" A wave of gratitude rushed through her. It was rare for Andy to call. He didn't have money to spend on long distance. He must have sensed that something big was happening in her life. Maybe there was some sort of ESP between them. After all, they were practically twins. "Oh Andy, I'm so glad you called. My mother's in the hospital! It might be the Plague."

"Geez, that's awful. Look, what did you tell Devon?"

"Mr. Devon?"

"About the bone marrow. He contacted me, and I figured he must have gotten in touch with you too."

So much for the ESP thing. She'd never believed in that anyway. "Andy, where are you?"

His answer came in a rush. "In San Francisco. I gotta talk fast. I'm at a pay phone and I don't have much change. Did Devon ask you for some bone marrow?"

"Yes, he said—"

Andy didn't let her finish. "Just don't do what he says, okay? Don't trust him."

"Andy, we're talking about my mother now! If she's got the Plague, and if my bone marrow can save her—"

He broke in again. "There's another way. I can't explain now, there's no time. I'm getting a bus to L.A. I'll be there in the morning. Just don't do anything till I get there. Are you at the hospital now?"

"Yes, but—"

"See if you can find something that tests for the Plague."

"Why?"

But the only response was a click, and then they were disconnected. Amy looked at the phone and mentally played back the conversation. In her panic, she'd almost forgotten about Mr. Devon's request. Now she was completely confused. On the one hand, maybe she wasn't as helpless as she thought she was. Her bone marrow might provide an antidote for her mother's condition. She didn't know much about bone marrow, but she did know it was powerful stuff. Her friend Chris had given bone marrow to the man he'd thought was his father, and it had saved the jerk's life.

But Andy had said Devon wasn't to be trusted. He'd said that before, and Amy hadn't always listened to him. But this time, he sounded so urgent, so sure of himself. And he had said he had an alternative.

Her phone rang again. "Hello, Andy?"

"This is Dr. Dave, Amy." He sounded very, very tired.

"What's going on?" she asked frantically. "How's my mother?"

"There's been no change," he said. He gave her the number of an office in the hospital and told her to meet him there.

He was sitting at a desk when she went in, and he managed a small smile. "I should have known you wouldn't stay home where you belong," he said.

"Do you know what's wrong with her?" Amy asked.

"Not yet."

"What happened?"

"She collapsed," he said simply. "I couldn't revive her, so I brought her here. Now we're running tests."

"Are you testing for . . ." She couldn't bring herself to say it. He finished the question for her.

"For the Plague? Yes, among other things. There's also the possibility that she has the flu, or maybe it was something she ate. It could even be sheer exhaustion."

"Or it could be the Plague," Amy said dully.

Dr. Dave had always been honest with her, and he didn't lie now. "Yes. It could be the Plague."

"When will you know for sure?"

"We've done the skin-patch test," he told her. "We'll see if there's a reaction in twenty-four hours." As he spoke, his eyes moved toward a small metal case. It was open, and Amy could see a stack of small, wrapped, white squares.

"Are those the test patches?" she asked.

"Yes."

"Tell me again how they work."

"It's quite simple. The patient wears the patch on an arm for a day. When it's taken off, if there's a pinkish red rash . . ."

"It's the Plague."

"Yes. But Amy, keep in mind that if your mother does have the Plague and we catch it immediately, there's a good chance—"

A nurse appeared at his door. "Dr. Hopkins, could

you come take a look at Mr. Collins in room four? I don't like the sound of his breathing."

"I'll be right there." He turned to Amy. "Why don't you go home? I'll call you when I have any news. Do you need money for a taxi?"

"No thanks, I'll be fine," Amy said. "Is it okay if I just sit here for a minute?"

"Sure, of course." Dr. Dave hurried off after the nurse.

Alone in the office, Amy couldn't take her eyes off the metal box. Andy had told her to find something that tested for the Plague, and there it was. Surely she could take one patch. Dr. Dave probably wouldn't even notice it was gone.

Or even more than one. She grabbed a handful out of the box and stuffed them in her pockets. She was stealing, she knew that. And she was stealing from a friend, which was even worse. But something in Andy's voice had told her this was important.

Another nurse appeared at the door. "What are you doing in here?" she demanded.

"Nothing," Amy said quickly. "I'm just leaving." And she did, trying very hard not to look as if she was carrying stolen goods.

f 5 ve

Alone at home that night, Amy didn't sleep well at all. Her worries about her mother kept waking her up, and even when she slept, the fears infected her dreams. She had the old nightmare, the one where she was trapped under glass as a fire raged around her. She knew it was a fragment of infant memory, of the time when she'd been growing in a laboratory incubator and the room had gone up in flames. Nancy Candler had rescued her.

But roles were reversed in the dream she had that night. Now it was her mother under the glass, and

Amy was the rescuer. But the dream Amy was an infant, not even a toddler. She could only crawl as she made her way into the fire, trying desperately to reach her mother, knowing all the time she didn't have the power to do anything to help her. Yet she kept on crawling, dragging her tiny body over the cold floor, through the hot flames. . . .

Relief flooded her body when a shrill noise jolted her out of her tormented sleep at five in the morning. She snatched up the phone by her bed.

"Hello? Hello?"

But there was only a dial tone. And the shrill noise continued, coming from somewhere else. Her cell phone? No, that played the Mexican Hat Dance.

She shook the last bits of sleep from her brain and realized that the noise was the doorbell. Jumping out of bed, she ran downstairs.

"Andy!"

"Hi."

"You look awful," Amy blurted out.

"Thanks a lot," he replied, and actually managed a crooked smile. She would have hugged him if she hadn't been so stunned by his appearance. His light hair hung in greasy, limp strings, there was bristle on his chin, and his clothes were rumpled and spotted. Plus, there was a certain odor emanating from him.

"Can I come in?" he asked. "I promise I won't touch anything."

"Of course," she said. Now that she could get a good look at him, she saw that he really seemed okay. He just hadn't bathed or washed his clothes for a while.

"What happened to you?" she asked.

He made a face. "*You* try sleeping three nights on buses, and benches in bus stations. And waking up to find someone's puked on you. Can I take a shower and wash my clothes?"

"Sure." She followed him up the stairs, keeping a safe distance behind. "What's going on? Where's Chris?"

"We split up in Seattle. He started hitchhiking east, to follow up on a lead we got about the organization. I was going to meet him in Chicago, but then I got that message from Devon when I checked my e-mail. So I knew I had to get out here fast, before you bought his story and started handing over your bone marrow."

"But what he said makes sense, Andy. If the Plague is genetic, and our genes aren't corrupted, we could provide a cure. We're talking about my *mother*, Andy! I'd risk anything for her."

"And I'm telling you that there's a better way to save her," Andy replied. "Wait till you hear me out." He stepped closer, and Amy stepped back.

"Take a shower first," she advised. "Throw your clothes into the hall and I'll put them in the wash. And I'll make you something to eat."

He gave her a real smile, and for the first time that morning she remembered how handsome he was. "That would be so great."

Thirty minutes later, a shiny, clean, sweet-smelling Andy was wrapped in a big bath towel, finishing a three-egg omelet and half a dozen link sausages. Amy transferred his clothes from the washing machine to the dryer. She called the hospital to check on her mother's condition—stable, no change—and sat back down at the kitchen table.

"Okay, tell me about your better way to stop the Plague," she ordered him.

"First of all, it's not *my* way. It comes from Singularity, Incorporated. You ever heard of them?"

"No."

"I found them on the Internet. It's a think tank right here in Los Angeles. A bunch of genius types who work on state-of-the-art science projects. They keep pretty much to themselves because they're dealing with some big ideas and they don't want publicity. And they don't want the government sticking its nose into their business. I've been exchanging e-mails with Howard, one of the guys there. They're all seriously cutting-edge. They've got a handle on really futuristic stuff."

"And they found a cure for the Plague?" Amy asked excitedly.

"No, but they've found a way to get the cure. Only they need people like us to do it for them."

"Why?"

"Because we're in perfect physical condition. Thanks to our genetic structure, we can withstand conditions normal humans can't."

"What kind of conditions?" she asked. "Weakness? Do they need our blood or some of our organs?"

"Not exactly. More like intense gravity. Traveling at the speed of light. That kind of thing."

Amy stared at him. "Andy, what in the world are you talking about?"

"Okay, I know it's going to sound crazy," Andy began. "Did Devon tell you about where the Plague comes from?"

"He said it's the result of genetic residue that was dormant, but it became active again."

"Right. And how did that genetic residue get into people in the first place?"

Amy recalled Devon's explanation. "It was millions of years ago. Some early humans came into contact with weird bacteria."

"Exactly. And that bacteria isn't anything we can get our hands on now. It's not indigenous to the planet. Maybe it was back then, but it's not anymore. So what we need is some of that original bacteria."

"And how are they going to get their hands on this bacteria if it doesn't exist anymore?"

"It can be extracted from the DNA of people who were infected. Not from the people who have it now, because the gene has mutated so much. It has to come from the source. Did you get something to test for the Plague?"

"Yeah, skin patches. They're in my backpack. But I'm not exactly sure I understand all this," Amy said.

Andy grinned. "Neither do I. But what it comes down to is this. The Singularity guys claim they can help us meet some of those original carriers. If we can get some skin cells or hair or something like that from them, doctors in the present will be able to cure the Plague."

"Andy, those first carriers lived thousands of years ago. I don't think we're going to find any of them hanging around today."

"I *know* that. We have to go back in time to find them. We test them with the patches, and get something like hair samples from the ones who are positive."

"Back in time," Amy echoed. Disappointment washed over her. "Time travel. What did this Howard tell you, that he's invented a time machine? And you believe him?"

"Look, I know it sounds crazy. And I can't explain it. I'm just asking you to come with me."

"Come with you *where*? The Stone Age?"

"No, to a building on Melrose. That's where the Singularity office is. Just listen to what these guys have to say."

Amy pushed away from the table. "I think your clothes are dry. You can put them on and get out of here. And I'll go give Mr. Devon a sample of bone marrow."

"Amy, no!" Andy jumped up and the towel started to slide off. Red-faced, he pulled it around himself more tightly. "Just think about this. It's not as crazy as it sounds. Even the laws of physics say it's possible to travel in time. If you travel at the speed of light, you can travel into the future."

"That's just a theory, Andy. Nobody's actually done it."

"You don't know that for sure," Andy replied. "If there's a fact-based theory, that means it can be done. You've heard of Albert Einstein, haven't you?"

Amy knelt down by the dryer and pulled out Andy's

clothes. "Yes, of course I've heard of Albert Einstein. And I know there are scientists who believe travel to the future can really happen. But not travel into the past, Andy, that's impossible. I've never heard anything about going backwards." She tossed Andy's clothes toward him. "Go get dressed."

"I'm staying right here," Andy said stubbornly. "I haven't finished talking to you."

Amy knew that tone of voice. With a sigh, she turned so her back was to him. "Okay, I won't look."

He continued to talk. "I can't explain it, Amy. I'm not a scientist. I don't even understand it. But I swear to you, these Singularity guys, they're for real. I did research. Important people have said they've got a grip on new technologies that no one else is dealing with."

"If they're so important, how come I've never even heard of them?" Amy asked.

"Like I said, they keep a low profile. And, okay, some scientists think they're a bunch of loonies. But I'll bet there were people who thought Albert Einstein was a loony too. Okay, you can turn around now."

She did. And despite her misgivings, a fully dressed and clean Andy inspired a confidence in her that she hadn't felt before.

He looked at her beseechingly. "Just come with me and hear what these guys have to say, okay?"

Maybe she was just too tired to argue anymore. Or maybe it was that golden glint in his eyes. In any case, Amy found herself giving in.

"Bring a toothbrush," Andy said. "Just in case." Within an hour, they were on Melrose, checking the numbers on the buildings.

"This is it," Andy said. It was a very ordinary-looking office building, and they entered a very ordinary-looking lobby. A bored security guard asked them where they were going.

"Singularity, Incorporated," Andy told him.

"Third floor, suite three-oh-two," the man intoned.

Amy wasn't sure what she had expected to find in the office of Singularity—incense and New Age music, maybe. Or a stark white laboratory filled with test tubes and bad smells. Instead, they found themselves in a room that looked like it could belong to an absent-minded professor: dusty, with lots of books, shabby furniture, magazines and newspapers piled on the floor. A man with long white hair and wire-rimmed glasses was sitting at a computer. A heavyset woman with bushy black curls and a multicolored Gypsy-style skirt was looking over his shoulder. They didn't exactly look like reputable scientists to Amy.

The woman looked up as they walked in. "Who are you?" she asked bluntly.

"My name is Andy Denker, and—"

The white-haired man jerked around. "Andy, hi! I'm Howard."

Amy couldn't help remembering a kindergarten classmate of hers named Howard. The other kids had teased him, calling him How-weird. The nickname would definitely be appropriate in this case. There was no way of telling how old the man was—somewhere between thirty and ninety was as close as Amy could get. He wore oversize patched blue jeans—not the fashionable hip-hop kind, just jeans that were way too big for him. A paper-thin T-shirt bore the words I WANT TO BELIEVE in faded black letters. An unlit cigarette dangled from the corner of his mouth.

He must have thought the cigarette was the cause of Amy's gaping. He took it out. "I quit three years ago," he told them. "I just like the feel of it."

The woman was appraising them. "So you're genetically designed clones," she said. "I'm Sarah." She began to walk around them, looking them up and down as if they were a couple of lab specimens. "Not bad. Not bad at all. Jimmy J did a good job."

"Who's Jimmy J?" Andy asked.

But Amy thought she knew. "Are you talking about Dr. Jaleski?"

"That's right," Sarah said. "Jimmy J, that was my nickname for him."

Amy tried to imagine anyone calling the dignified director of Project Crescent Jimmy J.

"Sarah gives everyone nicknames," Howard told them.

"What's yours?" Andy asked.

"How-weird."

Amy started laughing. The woman smiled back at her. "I like your necklace. I'll bet Jaleski made it for you."

Amy fingered the silver crescent-moon pendant that hung from the chain around her neck. "How did you know?"

"He was an old friend of ours," Sarah said. "We miss him."

Amy suddenly felt a warmth toward the woman. "So do I." Her eyes misted over as she remembered the kind man who had cared so much for humanity—and paid the price.

"I'll bet he'd approve of what you two are about to do," Howard declared.

Amy's eyes cleared. "Exactly what is it that we're about to do? If we agree to do it, that is."

"What do you know about space-time curvature?" Howard asked.

"Absolutely nothing," Amy replied promptly. She turned to Andy. "What about you?"

"Not much," he admitted. "Okay, I'll be honest. Absolutely nothing."

"Let me explain," Sarah said. "There is a region of space-time where the curvature becomes so strong that general relativity laws break down, and the laws of quantum physics—"

"Whoa!" Andy said. "You just lost me."

"Where?" Sarah asked.

Amy answered for both of them. "When you said, 'Let me explain.' Look, we do have superior intelligence, but we don't have any background in physics. I know most scientists agree that travel into the future is possible. But how can we go *back* in time?"

Howard jumped in. "It's easy! You just reverse the equation! You start off with relativity. . . ." He began scrawling numbers and letters on a blackboard. "And then you turn it around and do it backward instead of forward. You get another valid solution, see?"

"No," Amy said. For the first time in her life, she felt stupid. Fortunately, Andy looked just as blank as she did.

"Let me try," Sarah said. "You've heard of black holes, right?"

"It's a region of space that nothing can escape from," Andy said.

"Exactly. Well, the opposite would be a white hole, a region into which nothing can fall. The black hole sucks you in, the white hole spits you out."

"It doesn't sound like much fun," Amy remarked.

"Together, they make a wormhole," Howard said. "It's entering the wormhole that throws you into the future. The exit from the wormhole is in the past!"

Howard looked so pleased with himself that Amy hated to tell him she still didn't understand. "Maybe I'd better do some reading up on this," she said.

Sarah shook her head. "There's no time for that."

"We read very fast," Andy told her, but Sarah was still shaking her head. She looked at the clock on the wall.

"How much can you absorb in three minutes? Because that's when you have to leave. Otherwise, you'll miss the opening and it'll be at least two weeks before there's another opportunity. Do you think your mother can last that long? Or any of the other people who have the Plague? And how about all the people who could get it over the next fourteen days?"

Suddenly, Amy couldn't breathe. It finally hit her that these people were completely serious. They fully intended to send her and Andy into the past to help find a Plague antidote. They actually believed that they could do this. What was even more bizarre was the fact that she was beginning to believe it herself.

"We can do it, Amy," Andy said. "We're the only ones who can."

"He's right," Howard affirmed. He looked at the clock. "Less than three minutes. What do you say?"

"But—but . . ." Amy had a million questions. Like . . . "How do you know where we'll end up in time? And how are we going to get back?"

"It's all organized," Howard said. "Andy's got the details."

"But he doesn't understand this any more than I do!" Amy exclaimed.

"I don't have to understand to follow the directions," Andy said.

"Just keep this device with you at all times," Sarah said. She had picked up two shiny metallic buttons and pinned one to each of them. "It's a way for us to track you. We'll calculate the exact moment when you can be released from the wormhole, and we'll do it by remote control."

Amy turned to Andy. "We'll be together, right?"

"Absolutely," Andy said. But Amy caught the swift

glance that passed between Sarah and Howard. She stared at them long and hard.

"The thing is, we can't guarantee you'll be together," Howard admitted. "The portal might not admit both of you. Or you could get into the wormhole and find yourselves on different time planes."

"We have to risk it, Amy," Andy said. "This disease . . . it's the worst thing that's ever happened on this planet. It's bigger than your mother, you know. The Plague could wipe out the world."

She knew he wasn't exaggerating. And she knew they didn't have much time. She must have nodded, because they were instantly ushered into an adjoining room. A cylindrical contraption about the size of a phone booth stood in the center. The flick of a switch opened a huge skylight above it.

"We have twenty seconds," Sarah said. She opened the contraption and prodded Amy and Andy inside. It was a tight fit.

"And this thing is going to travel through space and time?" Amy asked doubtfully.

"No," Sarah said. "It stays right here and spins. You'll be ejected into the wormhole."

"Wait a minute," Amy cried out. "I don't like the sound of that—"

"There's no time to wait! Don't worry, I'd never hurt one of Jimmy J's clone babies!" And suddenly, the door closed.

"Ohmigod, Andy, what are we doing?" Amy moaned. It was pitch-black. She couldn't see a thing.

Andy took her hands, and they held on to each other tightly. The contraption began to move, slowly at first, then picking up speed. Amy hoped neither of them would get dizzy and throw up. That would be pretty disgusting in a space like this.

But she felt no dizziness as the contraption spun. In fact, she didn't feel anything. It was as if she had no body. She felt completely weightless, as if she was just floating in space. It was the oddest sensation— free-falling and being pulled toward something at the same time. All she was really aware of was the feeling of Andy's hands in hers.

Then she couldn't feel Andy's hands anymore. She couldn't feel her own breathing. She couldn't even feel her own emotions. She wasn't scared, which was a good thing . . . because she knew that at that moment she wasn't even human. She was some sort of pure energy, spinning in space. . . .

s i x 6

There was no abrupt thud, no sensation of crashing to earth. It was actually a pretty gentle transition. All that free-floating energy began to gel, becoming matter again. Slowly, Amy became aware of the bits and pieces of her physical being. She could curl her toes inside her shoes and feel the light brush of her hair against her cheek. All was black, but that didn't worry her. Sight would come back, along with everything else.

She had regained her sense of smell already—there was fresh air around her, the kind she never smelled in Los Angeles. At least, not in present-day Los Angeles.

She'd forgotten to ask if she'd be transported to the same place she'd left. There were a lot of questions she hadn't asked. But there hadn't been time.

She could hear a breeze rustling the trees. And she could touch. She put a hand to her face and felt her mouth, her nose, her eyes . . . and she realized her eyes were open. So why couldn't she see?

Because it's nighttime, dummy, Amy told herself. She tried speaking.

"Andy?"

It was a relief to hear her own voice. But it wasn't very comforting when she got no response. "Andy?" She could hear the quiver in her voice now.

Andy wasn't there. She was alone, totally, completely alone in a strange place, a strange time. Well, Sarah had said this might happen. Amy just hoped that wherever—*when*ever—Andy was, he was okay. Or were his atoms swirling around somewhere in space?

She couldn't think about possibilities like that. Andy was no dummy. He could take care of himself. And so could she.

Not to mention the fact that she had the entire population of twenty-first-century Earth—including her mother—to take care of too. She had a mission. And whatever time this was, there was certainly none to waste.

Amy opened her backpack and felt around inside. Her miniature flashlight was there somewhere . . . no, that was her toothbrush. There it was. She took it out and switched it on.

She was in a cave. It was small—stretching her arms, she could touch both sides, but she was able to stand up. Slowly, she moved around, holding the flashlight in front of her. The thin beam of light revealed an archway. She ducked under it and found herself outside.

It was lighter out there than in the cave. A huge, bright moon shone down, along with pinpoint lights that decorated the night sky. Stars, of course. Were there more stars back in the Stone Age? Maybe. Or maybe she could just see more because there were no lights shining on Earth.

There was no electricity in this world. No cars, no TVs, no phones . . . no indoor plumbing. Oh well, she'd gone camping in the wilderness before.

Her eyes had adjusted to the moonlight, and she could see pretty well now. Not that there was much to see—just trees and big rocks. She moved along, and a clearing came into view. There was a lake, and beyond that a mountain . . . no, it wasn't a mountain. It couldn't be a mountain. Because it was moving.

She rubbed her eyes and looked again. No, her vision was just fine. That great big dark form in the distance *was* moving. She strained her viewing power and tried to see the object in more detail. She made out a head, a body, a tail. . . .

It couldn't be. But it was. Way out there, ambling along as if it had every right to be there, was a dinosaur.

Pterodactyl? *Tyrannosaurus rex?* She didn't have the slightest idea. Even as a child, she hadn't been particularly interested in dinosaurs, certainly not to the extent of memorizing the different types like some kids did. She couldn't see the point of studying dinosaurs. After all, they weren't around anymore.

But they were *here,* in this time. And an even more chilling thought occurred to her. If dinosaurs roamed the earth, she wasn't back in the Stone Age. There were no signs of people around. It was only yesterday that she'd recited the words to Linda Riviera: Dinosaurs had died out sixty-five million years ago. The first humanlike beings appeared about three and a half million years ago. Sarah and Howard had miscalculated. They had sent her back sixty-one and a half million years too far.

Now she was upset. The risk she'd taken to come here—was it for nothing? If there were no humans, there was no one to test for the Plague. There was no DNA to collect. Unless it was the dinosaurs who were carrying the mutated gene. But then it wouldn't have shown up in humans. Humans didn't come from dinosaurs, they evolved from fish . . . or something. She wished she'd paid more attention in biology.

She touched the metal device that Sarah had pinned to her shirt. It was supposed to allow Singularity to track her. So by now, they should have figured out that she was in the wrong time, right? Or maybe not. Maybe she'd just have to hang out, keep herself hidden from the dinosaurs, and wait until the so-called think-tank guys decided she'd accomplished her mission. And they'd bring her back—with nothing to stop the Plague.

Her only optimistic thought was that maybe Andy had landed in the right time. As for herself, she would just crawl back to her cave and stay there till she was spit out of the wormhole. Thank goodness she'd thrown a bunch of nutrition bars into her pack.

She started to turn back. That was when her ear caught something. Real fear clutched her heart. Dinosaurs—and who knew what other kind of wild animals—were roaming this land. She was a genetically superior human being, but she was still a human being. There was no way she could defend herself against prehistoric creatures.

Her heart pounding, Amy strained to identify the sounds she was hearing. At first it was just noise, like groans and grunts. She'd never heard animal sounds like that before. And there was something else that surprised her. The sounds went up and down in tone. They weren't rhythmic—there was a burst of sound, then a brief silence, then two separate sounds, then a cough. A cough? Dinosaurs didn't cough, did they?

Then Amy heard something even more startling: laughter. And she knew she wasn't listening to animals.

There was still fear in her heart, but her curiosity was stronger. She began to move in the direction of the sounds, walking as quietly as possible. She didn't know what she would find. Some early form of human, perhaps, with some human characteristics, but wild and untamed. Beings that were more like animals than humans.

She was getting close to the sounds, and through some branches she saw a flicker of flame. She got down on her hands and knees and began to crawl. Keeping very still behind a large bushy growth, she pushed some thick branches aside and got a look at the source of the noises.

They were sitting around a campfire. She counted eighteen of them. There were males and females, all similarly clad in what looked like fur wraps and animal skins. The men had beards—at least, the older ones did. There were younger men too, and very young children. One woman held a baby in her arms.

One man was talking—at least, Amy guessed that was what the noises were. From the way everyone was paying attention, she got the feeling he was telling them a story. And it must have been a funny one, because when he paused, they all laughed.

Another man began to speak. His story wasn't funny—the members of the group looked serious. Others joined in, commenting on what they'd just heard. One man seemed pleased, another man less so. Their voices rose into what sounded like an argument. Not an actual fight, though. Just a debate. One man expressed concern about the first speaker's report of his encounter with an unusually large reptile. The other man thought the storyteller had made most of it up. After all, as everyone knew, he had a reputation for exaggerating.

Wait a minute. How did she know what they were saying? Why was it that she could suddenly make some sense out of the conversation?

Amy knew the answer. It was an aspect of her superior intelligence, the ability to learn a language quickly. That was what was happening—she was learning their language as they spoke.

The large group broke into smaller groups. Three girls who looked to be about Amy's age huddled together and talked quietly among themselves. She couldn't hear what they said, but they were giggling in a way that made her think they were talking about boys. The woman with the baby was asking another woman about *her* children. And the man who'd told the funny story was asking if anyone wanted something. . . . Fruit? Nuts? She strained to hear, but she was distracted by a tickling on her hand.

She turned and found herself eye to eye with something she couldn't identify. Something large, on four legs, with fierce eyes. Her natural impulse took over—and she shrieked. The creature ran away.

But now, eighteen other pairs of eyes were looking in her direction. Some of them rose and started moving toward her. As they approached, their eyes looked even fiercer than the creature's.

se7en

If the look in their eyes wasn't scary enough, the fact that at least half of them were carrying spears definitely was. Amy considered her options. She could probably outrun them, but if their spear-throwing techniques were halfway decent, she'd be dead. Scramble up a tree? No, she'd be stuck there, and even more vulnerable to their attack.

Amy told herself they only looked fierce and threatening because they didn't know what was lying in wait for them in the bushes. So before they could start throwing their spears, she stood up and revealed herself to them. One look at small-boned thirteen-going-on-fourteen Amy Candler and they lowered their spears.

The three girls her own age immediately started giggling. One of the larger men came forward and spoke. It was amazing how the harsh noises had become comprehensible words to her.

"Who are you? Where do you come from?"

Would speaking the language come as easily to her as understanding it? Sometimes she overestimated her own amazing abilities to learn faster than any normal beings. But not this time. Her mouth moved and her voice formed the guttural sounds.

In their tongue, she said, "I am Amy. I come from . . ." She hesitated.

The woman with the baby seemed concerned. "Are you lost?"

"Yes," Amy replied.

Another woman spoke. "You are not one of the others?"

Amy had no idea who the others were, but she got the feeling that the woman didn't care for them, whoever they were. "No. I am not one of the others."

"What tribe do you belong to?" another man asked.

"I'm . . . I'm an American," she said lamely.

"I do not know this tribe," the man said. "It must be far from here."

"Yes," Amy said. "Very, very far."

A woman with a kind smile stepped forward. "Then you are tired and hungry. Come sit with us."

Amy pushed her way through the bushes and entered the clearing. She followed the woman, passing the younger girls, who were staring at her. One of them whispered to the other two, and they all started giggling again. Amy had a feeling they were laughing at her clothes.

How rude, she thought, but she couldn't blame them. They'd never seen jeans, T-shirts, backpacks . . . not to mention shoes. Still, their mocking laughter made her blush. If a girl showed up at Parkside wrapped in the skin of some spotted animal, *Amy* wouldn't make fun of her. Mainly because she'd think it was the latest look. Except, of course, for the fact that it was totally uncool to wear the skin of an animal.

But one look around the group told her this was definitely not a fur-free society. Wearing fur was considered inhumane where she came from, but here nobody had invented fake fur yet. Or fake anything. She noticed that the coronet in the hair of the woman she sat by was made of real leaves and red berries.

"Pretty," Amy said, pointing to the coronet, and the woman said, "Thank you." Behind her, the girls were giggling harder now. Obviously, Amy had just done or said something they thought was stupid.

Another woman approached with a stick. On the end of the stick was a charred hunk of meat, and the woman offered it to Amy.

It didn't smell half bad—kind of like barbecued pork. But Amy was nervous. She remembered smelling something good in Paris, taking a bite, and finding out it was a snail. She'd been tormented, wanting to spit it out but afraid of insulting the French people around her.

Amy accepted the meat and took a tentative bite. She couldn't identify it, but it was good, sort of spicy. Her curiosity must have been evident, because the woman pointed to it and said a word. Amy had no idea what it meant, but she smiled and nodded as she chewed.

Now the group began what seemed to be a ritual. One by one, each person sitting around the fire recounted his or her activities of the day. Concentrating, Amy was able to make out some parts of the stories. A woman talked about scraping a skin to make a roof for a shelter. A man announced that his son had killed his first deer. The teenage boy rose and accepted congratulations, and Amy tried to erase the image of Bambi's mother from her mind.

A woman reported on the gathering of fruit, while another expressed disappointment in the poor selection of nuts she had found. Three men had located a stream where fish appeared to be plentiful, and they promised the group there would be a big fish dinner the next night. Another man recounted his efforts to hunt down a bear.

Even the teenage girls had a report—something about egg gathering. By this time, Amy had figured out that she was in a society of hunters and gatherers. There was cooked food, and they spoke of houses, and they had the big noses and heavy brows she remembered from a picture in her science book, so these folks were probably what her textbook called Neanderthals. That meant she'd traveled back in time anywhere from two hundred thousand to thirty thousand years. So why were dinosaurs still hanging around?

Maybe she'd made a mistake, and that wasn't a dinosaur she'd seen earlier. Just some big old woolly mammoth thing. It was just her imagination playing tricks.

But *this* wasn't her imagination. This was real. She was sitting around a campfire with a bunch of Neanderthals. Wait till Tasha heard about this. And her mother . . .

Thinking of her mother made her remember why

she'd come here in the first place. She looked around for her backpack.

"Hey! What are you doing?"

At least two of the girls had the courtesy to look embarrassed by the fact that they'd been caught going through Amy's backpack. The third one, whose reddish brown hair was twisted in ropy dreadlocks, pushed the pack aside and gave her a challenging look.

"Does this belong to you?" she asked with phony innocence.

"Yes. You know that, you saw me carry it."

Dreadlocks shrugged. "I was not interested in you, so I did not notice what you carried. I gave no attention to you at all."

"Then why were you laughing at me?" Amy asked. "You must have noticed something."

The short girl, who had straight black hair that fell to her eyes, laughed. "She is correct, Lulu." Or at least that's what the name sounded like. She turned back to Amy. "We all watched you. I am Reena."

"Hello, Reena. My name is Amy."

"Yes, we heard you say that." She indicated the third girl, who had an unruly mop of blond curls. "This is . . ." The sounds that made up the third girl's name were impossible for Amy to say, so she just smiled and said, "Hello, it's nice to meet you." She noticed that her makeup bag was open and a lip gloss had fallen out.

"Do you know what this is?" she asked the girls. She opened the tube and twisted the stick of color out.

"Paint!" Reena said. "But I have never seen a color like that. What kind of plant does this paint come from?"

"It doesn't come from a plant," Amy said.

"It is a berry paint," Lulu said.

"Well, no, not exactly, you see—"

But Lulu apparently did not like to be contradicted. "It is ugly," she declared flatly.

The girl with the blond curls and the unpronounceable name tugged on Amy's jeans. "What animal does this come from?"

Amy was about to tell her that denim didn't come from an animal, but then she remembered that denim is cotton and cotton comes from—

"It comes from a plant," she said. They looked blank. "It is made from a plant that grows near my home."

"It is ugly," Lulu said flatly.

Reena picked up a plastic case. "This is what?"

Amy had no idea how to explain plastic, so she opened it and showed them the blue eye shadow inside. "Paint for eyelids."

Lulu sneered at it while the third girl and Reena oohed and ahhed. "May I try this?" Reena asked.

"Sure," Amy said. "I'll show you how." She rubbed a finger in the blue powder and instructed Reena to close her eyes.

"How does this look?" Reena asked Curl Girl.

"Very pretty," she said, but Lulu made a noise that clearly indicated her displeasure.

"Do you have a mirror?" Amy asked Reena.

"A what?"

Stupid question. "Oh, that's like . . . water. In a lake. Where you can see yourself."

"What is this?" Curly asked. She had pulled out the metal case holding the patches.

"Oh, please don't touch that!" Amy cried out. Her distress interested Lulu, who proceeded to grab the case from Curly. She shot Amy a triumphant look as she got the case open.

Curly and Reena examined the white squares. "Is it a decoration for the body?" Reena asked.

"No, it's . . ." And then Amy realized this was a perfect opportunity to start her Plague testing. "Yes! It is a decoration. It is very popular in my tribe. Would you like to wear one?" She peeled off the backing and placed the patch on Reena's arm. Then she did the same for Curly.

She could see Lulu watching the procedure with

interest, but when Amy turned to her, she pretended to yawn.

"Would you like a decoration too?" Amy asked.

"No. It is ugly." With that, Lulu rose and stomped off. Apparently, she was the leader of the pack, since Reena and Curly immediately jumped up and took off after her.

The group around the campfire was breaking up. The woman with the leaves in her hair took Amy to a tentlike structure made of branches, with some sort of animal hide tossed over the top for a roof. Apparently this was the tribal guest room.

Fumbling in her backpack, Amy took out her toothbrush and tried to remember which direction the lake was in. Then she decided she was too tired to brush her teeth. After all, she'd traveled thousands of years; she was entitled to one night with unbrushed teeth.

Maybe it was her teeth that kept her from sleeping well. Or it might have been the cold dirt floor, or the fur blanket that still smelled of some poor animal's blood. Or it could have been jet lag. In any case, a very slight rustling in her tent caused her to sit right up— just in time to see the glint of the metal case as someone took it away.

Amy ran out after the thief. Under the light of the

moon, she identified the fleeing figure. It was Lulu, clutching the metal box with the precious patches inside. Amy was gratified to realize that going back to the Stone Age hadn't affected her athletic skills. Lulu was a fast runner, but Amy was easily able to catch up to her.

She grabbed the girl's arm. "Give me that box!"

Lulu pushed her away, and Amy tripped. On the ground, she looked up at Lulu in fury and scrambled to her feet. Before Lulu could turn to run, Amy pushed *her* down and straddled her.

Strangely enough, Lulu didn't struggle. She was very still, staring at something behind Amy, and her mouth was open, as if she was uttering a silent scream.

Amy knew that trick. Lulu was expecting Amy to turn around, and then she'd take off again. Amy refused to fall for it. "Oh, stop that, there is nothing behind me," she snapped.

She was wrong. And when the huge mouth caught her at the waist, it was too late to do anything.

She felt herself rising. She watched Lulu get smaller, and the fear that filled her was unlike anything she'd ever felt before. She couldn't see what held her, but she could feel its strength, and there was no way she could fight it. Higher and higher she rose. Whatever creature had her in its grasp, it was about to devour her, and the horror of it was unspeakable.

She could see its feet now—huge webbed things. Lulu was a speck on the ground. But even in this moment of utter despair, Amy's vision didn't fail her. She saw the little speck plunge toward the creature's webbed feet.

The creature roared, and suddenly, Amy was falling. She'd fallen or jumped from high places before. She knew how to land to suffer the least trauma. Still, when she hit the ground, she was momentarily stunned. She knew she should move, run, but the extreme shock of the experience paralyzed her.

Lulu was still there. She knelt by Amy's side. "You can rest now. It is gone."

Amy struggled to a sitting position. She looked and saw the creature's back, now far from them. But not so far that Amy couldn't identify it.

"It was a dinosaur," she murmured.

"Is that what your people call them?" Lulu asked. "Dinosaur?"

"Yes." But how could it be? Everything she'd read had been very clear—the dinosaur had disappeared from earth long, long before the Neanderthals.

"Do you see many of these dinosaurs where you come from?" Lulu wanted to know.

"No. None at all."

"We see very few," Lulu said. "Our storytellers say

that at one time they were running wild all over the land. It is rare that we see a wild one now. Is this the first you have seen?"

"Yes," Amy said faintly. "And I hope it's the last." So the textbooks and encyclopedias were wrong. She'd wondered how they could be so absolutely positive about something that had happened before writing was invented. There was no way anyone could know for sure exactly when the last dinosaur died.

She looked at Lulu. "You saved my life."

Lulu shrugged, but even in the dim light Amy could see the pink in her cheeks. Emboldened, Amy asked, "Could I tell this story at the campfire tomorrow night?" She had a feeling that being described as a hero was a pretty big deal around here.

"But then you would have to explain why you were chasing me," Lulu said. She picked up the metal box lying on the ground nearby.

"I won't tell them you took my box," Amy said.

Lulu uttered the word for *thank you* and handed Amy the box. Now it was Amy's turn to express gratitude, but it was for a lot more than the return of the Plague patches.

Together, Amy and Lulu walked back toward the settlement. They said nothing, but a bond existed between them now. Amy knew she wouldn't have to suffer any more taunts from the girl.

When they reached the guest tent, Amy opened the box. "Would you like a decoration now?" she offered.

"Yes. Will you show me how to wear it?"

Lulu watched as Amy peeled off the backing and stuck the patch on her arm. Lulu smiled.

"I was lying when I said it was ugly," she confided. And she ran off.

e8ght

When she woke up in the morning, it took Amy a minute to remember where she was. Once that was established in her head, she became aware of how grubby she felt. She'd slept in her clothes, she hadn't brushed her teeth—and she was in major need of a shower.

Of course, a shower was not an option in the Stone Age. But Amy remembered the lake she'd seen when she first arrived. She headed in that direction, keeping an eye out for dinosaurs along the way.

Once she had reached the lake without encountering

any nasty beasts, or any humans, she peeled off her clothes and ran into the water.

It felt wonderful! Clear, and deliciously clean, not at all like the so-called freshwater lakes she'd known back home. There was nothing in this world to pollute this water. There were no fumes from cars, no chemicals . . . the water was truly fresh. She splashed, she swam, she dove and saw brilliantly colored fish.

When she returned to the surface, she heard familiar giggles. Lulu, Reena, and Curly were standing on the bank, watching her. And she had no clothes on. *This* was really embarrassing. Self-consciously, with her arms folded across her chest, she came out of the lake and hurried toward the clothes she'd left lying in the dirt.

She felt so fresh and clean that she hated the idea of putting her jeans and T-shirt back on. As it turned out, she didn't have to.

"We have brought you something," Lulu announced, and Reena presented a length of leopard skin.

Amy uttered a silent apology to her mother, who would be furious at the thought of Amy's wearing animal fur. "Thank you." She accepted the fur, and the girls helped her wrap it in the way they wore theirs. For the first time ever, Amy understood why the kids at her own school dressed pretty much alike. It felt good to belong.

"Will you come and gather eggs with us?" Lulu asked. Amy agreed, and the girls started walking.

"My father says that the birds have been plentiful at the rim of the valley," Curly announced.

"I would prefer to examine the nests in the trees by the wide river," Lulu declared.

"But there are only a few trees in that area," Curly argued. "I do not think we will find many eggs."

Reena laughed. "Silly girl! By the river, we can find something much more interesting than eggs!"

When they arrived at the river, Amy saw what she meant. Three teenage boys holding long harpoons stood in the knee-deep water, spearing fish. Clearly, that was the reason why the girls wanted to hang out there. Amy was reminded of her friends who always seemed to find an errand to run in the vicinity of a certain video arcade because that was where the boys were. Things hadn't changed much in thousands of years.

Pretending not to notice the boys, who were looking at *them,* the girls climbed trees and searched for nests. And talked, of course.

"My sister admired my new decoration," Reena said. "She wants to have one too."

"I have lots of them," Amy assured her. And when the tribe gathered for a meal a short time later, she passed them around.

"Are you going to give patches to *everyone*?" Lulu asked in dismay.

Amy knew why Lulu didn't want her giving them out. If everyone wore them, they wouldn't be cool. Still, she had to test as many people as possible. As she was showing them how to peel off the backings, an older man had a question for her.

"Is this a gift of your tribe?"

"Yes, sort of."

"Then we must present you with gifts to take back to your people." A few moments later, she saw him put on an amazing head covering. It was some sort of cap with antlers from a deer. Now *that* would be a souvenir.

"Nice hat!" she exclaimed. "Can I get some of those to take with me?"

A shocked silence fell over the group. The man with the antlers glared at her. Lulu hurried to her side.

"He is the leader of our tribe," she whispered. "The only person who can wear that. It will bring our men good luck in the hunt."

Amy apologized profusely, and the leader softened. "You come from a primitive tribe," he said. "This is not your fault. But if you stay with us, you must learn to accept our ways."

"I will," Amy promised.

But the ways of the Stone Age were not easy. There was no school, which was nice, but instead, there was pelt scraping. The women and girls spent hours cleaning fresh skins. Amy was given a rock that had been sharpened to make an almost razorlike edge. The smell of the skin alone made her want to gag.

"You do this every day?" she asked Lulu.

"Most days," Lulu replied. "When there is a good hunt. Today we will eat the meat of this panther. This skin will become clothing. It is disgusting."

"I'm glad you think so too," Amy said. She was beginning to understand why people became vegetarians.

"No one wears panther anymore," Lulu told her. "It is . . ." And here she used a word Amy didn't know. It was easy enough to guess its meaning, though. Something like *uncool*.

After the pelt scraping came the nut gathering. This was followed by berry picking. That was when Amy had her next truly frightening encounter. True, the long, fat snake wasn't the size of a dinosaur. But she'd never seen a snake so big before. As it hissed and slithered toward her, moving really fast, Amy felt almost as much fear as she had upon seeing the dinosaur. She leaped onto the closest tree and climbed rapidly. The snake climbed after her.

Once again, she was rescued. Lulu and the other girls began throwing rocks at the snake. Not until it fell from the tree and lay still on the ground did Amy dare climb back down.

"What is that called?" she asked, her voice shaking.

"Lunch," Curly told her. Sure enough, at the break for the midday meal, Amy watched without any appetite as the snake was cut into chunks and turned into something like kabobs.

"Do you really *eat* that?" she asked Lulu.

"Of course! You ate it last night!"

Amy tried to keep her reaction to herself. Snails in France, snake in the Stone Age . . . She supposed she should appreciate the fact that she was experiencing the cuisine of a new culture. Or an old one.

After lunch, there was more work, searching for certain plants and roots. It dawned on her that she'd been working exclusively with women all day. "Where are the men and the boys?"

"Hunting and fishing," Lulu told her.

So her textbook was correct on that topic. "Men are the hunters and women are the gatherers."

"Is it not the same among your people?" Reena asked.

"No, we choose what we want to do," Amy replied.

The women seemed startled, and Amy wondered if she should plant the seeds of feminism among them. But something distracted her.

"Ohmigod, look!" she screamed. "It's another dinosaur!"

The others turned in the direction she was pointing. Lulu put an arm around her. "That is a tame dinosaur. He cannot hurt you. He is used for transportation."

Amy gaped. "You mean like in *The Flintstones*?"

"Where are the Flintstones?"

"They're just . . . they're some people back home." Amy couldn't wait to report that a dumb cartoon actually showed images of Stone Age life as it really was.

When the long workday was over, she helped Lulu carry stuff back to the cave her family called home. There, Lulu and her mother separated and organized the various plants, and Amy admired the murals on the cave walls. The pictures showed the cavepeople engaged in various activities—mainly hunting and gathering, of course.

Lulu was searching for something. "Mother, where is my horse-tooth necklace?"

Lulu's mother answered in the same way Amy's mother would have. "Where did you leave it?"

"Right here, by my sleeping mat. And it is not here now." She frowned. "It has been stolen."

Amy supposed theft had to be a big problem in this community. After all, there was no way to lock a cave. But when she inquired about this, Lulu's mother was offended.

"Our people do not steal from each other," she informed Amy.

"It must have been the others," Lulu said darkly.

Amy recalled having heard about them the day before. "Who are these others? A tribe?"

"Yes." Lulu wrinkled her nose. "A very different tribe. Not like us."

"They are not friendly," her mother said. "They watch us, but they do not speak to us. They come from far away, I believe."

"Are they dangerous?" Amy asked.

"No," Lulu said. "But our people have found them in our caves, looking at our things, touching our things. They make marks with sticks on thin, white skins."

"That's weird," Amy said. She wouldn't mind checking out these others—if she had time. It was so interesting being here, she kept forgetting that her visit had a purpose. That night she would look under the patches worn by Lulu, Curly, and Reena. If they showed no skin reaction, she would give out the remainder of the patches. By the next night, she hoped to be home.

It was amazing how quickly she was adjusting to the Stone Age. So far, she wasn't missing any modern technologies. In the hour before dinnertime, when she would normally have been watching TV, she was outside with the tribe, collecting wildflowers.

Reena was trying to put a flower in her hair, but it fell out. "I hate my hair," she said. "It is so heavy on my head. And it falls in my eyes."

Amy wanted to suggest cutting it, but she knew they had no scissors, and the sharp stones they used to cut skins probably wouldn't work well on hair. She considered describing the way a pair of scissors worked. She could even help them make some. Then she recalled something she had learned from reruns of *Star Trek*.

Mr. Spock always talked about something called the Prime Directive. When the *Enterprise* visited primitive cultures, the crew wasn't supposed to introduce anything modern that would change the culture's natural progress. Anything Amy did now could affect the future of the world. She had to be very careful.

But Reena kept moaning and groaning about her messy hair, and Amy felt so sorry for her, she asked, "Have you ever considered braiding it?"

The girls had never heard of braiding, so Amy demonstrated how to twist locks of hair to get them out of the way. She was probably disobeying the Prime Directive, but she didn't think braids would change the course of the universe.

When it was time for the tribe to gather for dinner, Amy went back to her tent to get the patches. But the metal box was nowhere to be seen.

She went back to join her girlfriends. "Did you take the rest of my patches?"

"No. Why do you think I would take them?"

"Because you don't want me to give them to everyone."

"I do not care about that anymore," Lulu said. "You can have mine back."

"Yes, I am tired of mine too," Reena said. They both pulled off their patches, and so did Curly.

It seemed that fashion trends had about the same life span in the Stone Age as they had at Parkside Middle School. Amy was more interested in checking out the skin that had been under the patches.

There were no rashes. She absolutely needed to test more people. "I have to find the rest of the patches. Do you think an animal might have taken the box?" She snapped her fingers. "I know! What about the others? You said they take things."

"This is possible," Lulu said, and the other two girls agreed.

"I want to go look for them," Amy said. "Will you come with me?"

They all looked horrified. As it turned out, they weren't afraid of the others. Instead, the others appeared to be the Stone Age equivalent of nerds and losers, and the girls refused to be seen near them.

At least they were willing to point Amy in the right direction.

n**9**ne

Amy had been told that the others lived beyond the ridge and on the opposite side of a wide valley. If she walked normally, it would take her forever to get there. Fortunately, no one was around, and she could run at high speed. Even so, it took more than an hour before she reached the area across the valley.

But she saw no tents, no inhabited caves, no signs of a campfire. She realized she must be only on the outskirts of the community. She was hungry, tired, and in a very bad mood. By the time she returned to *her* tribe, the people would have finished eating dinner and telling their stories. She'd have to wait until the next day's first meal to get patches on people, and then another day before she could check the results.

She plodded along, searching the area for the so-called others. In her mind, she envisioned a group of slovenly, degenerate types lazing around and doing nothing. So when she saw a young man industriously chopping wood, she wondered if perhaps she'd come upon the wrong settlement.

The instrument he was using to chop the wood looked like a real ax. She hadn't seen anything like that back in the other settlement. Then the boy did something that surprised her even more. He put down the ax, and from a pocket in the belt around his waist, he drew out what looked like paper and a pencil. He wrote something down, and then he put the paper and pencil back into the pocket.

He had some sort of fur hat on his head, and he didn't hear her approach. She only got a glimpse of his face, but she was impressed. He was clean-shaven—and cute.

"Hello."

His head jerked up. He was clearly startled to see her, and he didn't respond.

"Hello," she said again.

His eyes darted around, as if he was seeking help.

She wondered if perhaps he spoke a different language. "Do you understand me?"

"No," he said.

She looked at him skeptically. "Then how did you know what I just asked you?"

He began tossing logs into something that looked like a wheelbarrow. Amy stared at the contraption. "What's that? I didn't think the wheel was invented yet."

He grabbed the handles of the wheelbarrow and began to roll it away. Amy hurried after him. "Hey, wait! I'm talking to you! Don't walk away from me!" But the boy kept going, picking up his pace.

"Stop!" she shrieked.

When he didn't, she ran and jumped him from behind.

He fell to the ground, and she held him there. He looked desperate. "Do not speak to me. I am stupid. Slow. No brain."

"You know what a brain is?" He realized his error and closed his eyes. That's when she noticed what lay by the wheelbarrow. She picked it up. "This looks like a book!"

"Book?" he repeated nervously. He struggled to free himself, but he was no match for her.

"Are you from the future?" she demanded. "Answer me! What is your name?"

He groaned. She could see in his eyes that he was about to give up.

"You took my patches, didn't you?"

"Me, no," he gasped.

"You, yes," she insisted.

"No, that is my name. Meno. Could you get off of me, please? I won't run."

"You'd better not," she said. "I'll just come after you." She released him. He sat up, rubbing his arms where she'd held him down and looking at her ruefully.

Now she could see that he wasn't much older than she was. "You're not one of them, are you?" she asked.

"One of who?" he asked nervously.

"One of *them*." She cocked her head in the direction she'd come from. "The Neanderthals."

He shook his head.

"You're like me. You come from the future, right?"

His eyes widened. "You come from the future?"

She was taken aback. His reaction was honest; she could see the awe in his expression. But he *had* to be from the future! He could read and write, and he had equipment that didn't belong in this age. He was more sophisticated in every way.

"Meno!" An older man was approaching them. He

didn't look pleased at the sight of the boy with Amy. Meno scrambled to his feet.

"Yes, Father."

Amy stepped forward boldly. "I am Amy. I am looking for a box. It is made of metal."

"We do not have your metal box," the man said.

"But you know what metal is?" she asked.

The man's face hardened. "Come, Meno."

Meno shot Amy a look that was almost apologetic. Then he grabbed the handles of the wheelbarrow and followed his father.

Amy waited until they were almost out of sight in the surrounding forest. Then she went after them. Keeping her distance, she crept along silently and tried to hear what they were saying. She made out sounds, but they weren't the same sounds she and Meno had been making a few minutes before. Meno and his father were speaking another language.

She uttered a silent groan. This was the last thing she wanted to do—learn another language. Learning might come a lot easier to her than to ordinary people, but it was still work, and she'd been working all day. She was tired, hungry, frustrated, and worried about her mother.

But she persevered, and grimly concentrated, and ultimately, she managed to pick up on some of the conversation. Actually, it wasn't a conversation. In a conversation at least two people participated. This was a lecture. Meno's father did all the talking.

He was saying something like "You must not communicate with them" and "We cannot let them know who we are." It sounded as though he thought Amy was one of the Neanderthals, and Meno was saying nothing to contradict him. Which was interesting . . .

Where were they going? She still hadn't seen any signs of a dwelling, or any other people, for that matter. Meno and his father were moving more slowly now, as if their destination was at hand. But Amy saw nothing lying ahead of them. They arrived at a small clearing in the woods and stopped. They seemed to be waiting.

Amy edged as close as she could and ducked behind a tree. There she waited and strained to pick up more of the father's lecture. She began to understand. Now what the father said made sense. Terrible sense.

"Remember why we are here, my son. We are planning to colonize this planet. These people . . . if they fight, they will die. If they submit, we will allow them to live in peace, but this will no longer be their land. You must not attempt any friendship with these people. If they know where we are from, they will be frightened. They cannot possibly understand. You must accept this, my son. You will have no relationship with the natives."

Amy couldn't hear Meno's response. He and his father were suddenly surrounded by a beam of light. As Amy watched in disbelief, they began to rise from the ground. The beam was like an elevator, lifting them. She could just make out where they were going. It was only a speck, way up in the sky, but she could see what it was. A huge, round, shiny spaceship.

ten 10

Amy didn't go back to the Neanderthals that night. She picked up leaves and piled them in a thick mound to use as a bed. To curb the hunger pangs, she gathered nuts and berries that she recognized from collecting she'd done with the tribe. And for entertainment, she had the book that Meno had left behind. She curled up in her leaves with her back against the trunk of a tree and tried to read.

It wasn't easy. Even after she was able to interpret the symbols that constituted words and letters, the book was impossible to comprehend. It was a weird mixture of science and philosophy, and it was way over her head. Whoever those people in the spaceship were, they were very smart. But that didn't give them the right to take over a planet.

She slept fitfully. Every time the wind blew, she woke with a start, expecting to see a beam of light. Or a large snake. Or a dinosaur. When she finally did fall into a real, deep sleep, it was almost dawn. Maybe that was why the beam of light didn't wake her. Meno's voice did that.

"Amy."

She opened her eyes.

"That's your name, isn't it? I heard you say it to my father."

She sat up and rubbed her eyes. "Yes. That's my name."

"I, um, I just wanted to apologize for running out on you," he said. "And I had to ask you . . . are you really from the future?"

"Yes," she said. "Are you really some sort of alien who plans to colonize the planet?"

He was stunned. "How did you know that?"

"I followed you and your father. I heard what your father said."

"But we were speaking in our language! How did you understand him?"

"I'm a fast learner."

He was intrigued. "Is this something people in the future will be able to do? Learn entire languages so quickly?"

"Not all people," she said. "I'm special. But I don't want to talk about me. I want to know what you guys think you're doing! You can't just walk onto a planet and claim it for yourself!"

Meno was surprised by her sudden attack. "Look, I don't know what it's like where you're from. These people here are primitive."

"Of course they're primitive," Amy said. "They haven't been around very long."

"They don't have a real language, not the kind you can read or write. They don't even know how to count! You know what they say if you ask them how many people are in their tribe? 'A lot!' "

"So what?" Amy responded. "They'll learn how to count eventually. And they'll make languages, lots of them, and they'll write books and everything. I'm from their future and I can guarantee you, we've got it all."

"How far into the future did you come from?" Meno asked.

"About a quarter of a million years."

Meno was intrigued. "Tell me about the future."

It seemed natural then to start walking. As they ambled through the forest, Amy told him about life on

Earth as she knew it. Not the bad stuff, of course. As a representative of her century, she wanted to stress the positive. So she didn't tell him about wars, or the state of the environment, or poverty, or hunger. She talked about cars and planes, TV and telephones and computers—that sort of thing.

But Meno wasn't impressed. "We've got all that stuff right now."

That was interesting. "So, if you take over the planet, humans wouldn't have to wait thousands of years for something to read."

Meno nodded. "We'll give them everything now."

"But that's not the way it's supposed to be," Amy argued. "They—we—humans have to grow at their own rate. And just because they're not as advanced doesn't mean they don't have the right to their own planet. They have to be left alone so they can evolve."

"My father says that could take hundreds of thousands of years," Meno said.

"So what?" Amy asked. "They don't look like they're in a big rush."

Meno was silent for a moment. "How long have you been here, anyway?"

Amy admitted she was a recent arrival to the Stone Age.

"We've been here for almost a year," Meno told her.

"Watching them, studying them. We know more about their race than they know. We've been able to reshape our own physique to look like them so we wouldn't frighten them when we arrived."

She wondered what Meno *really* looked like. It was clear to her that his people had modeled themselves after the ideal of human—Neanderthal—appearance.

"That's nice of you," Amy said. "But what you guys are doing here, it's wrong." She frowned. "How can I explain it?"

"You don't have to," Meno said. "I understand. I even agree with you."

She stopped walking. "You do?"

He looked miserable. "I've been telling my father this ever since we arrived. I've told all of them, the high council, *everyone*. We shouldn't be interfering with the natural development of a civilization."

"Exactly!" Amy exclaimed. "It's against the Prime Directive!"

"The *what*?"

Obviously they didn't get *Star Trek* reruns on his planet. "Never mind," she said, and they continued to walk. "What did your father say?"

"Nothing. He won't listen."

"You've got to *make* him listen!"

"I can't," Meno said.

"Look, you have to do something to stop them!"

"Like what?"

"I don't know. Something!"

"I can't do anything. You should understand that. I'm just a kid, like you."

"Don't compare yourself to me," Amy said huffily. "I've traveled back thousands of years to find a cure for the Plague and save my mother. And save the world too!"

It was his turn to stop suddenly. "Really? You're doing that all on your own?"

"Yes." She told him about the disease, and how it had been traced to a primitive gene. Which meant she had to explain about herself and her superior genes. This made him feel a little better.

"So you're not an ordinary kid. See, I'm just ordinary for my people. I can't change anything. I'm not special."

Amy looked at him sternly. "You can be special if you want to be. You can save the human race, just like I'm doing."

"But what can I do?" he asked plaintively.

"I don't know!" She looked up at the spaceship. "Those are your people, not mine. You have to figure it out. But mainly, you can't give up!"

Now he was looking up at the spaceship too.

"Go back up there," she urged. "Demand that they listen to you."

He was considering it, she could tell. "And while you're up there," she said, "look around for a metal box."

His face was grim. "You're right. I have to keep trying. If you can try to save the human race, so can I." He started back to the clearing where he had arrived. Amy walked alongside him.

"That's the spirit!" she said encouragingly. "And if your father won't listen to reason, then—then make something up! Tell him you're homesick and you want to go home. Or tell him if he doesn't listen, you'll get a complex and have a nervous breakdown or something like that. Tell him you'll lose all your self-esteem. Here on Earth, they make a big deal about kids needing self-esteem. At least, in *my* time they do."

They were back where they had started. Meno took some sort of remote-control device from his pocket and pressed a button. Within seconds the white beam of light came down from the spaceship.

His expression both grim and determined, he stepped into the light.

"Don't forget my metal box!" Amy called.

He didn't seem to hear her.

"Meno! Did you hear me?"

He looked at her vaguely. "What?" He was already beginning to rise.

She might never have another chance. She jumped into the light and began rising with him.

eleven

It was smoky in the beam of light. When the smoke cleared, Amy found herself by Meno's side in a shiny, empty room. He was not happy to see her there.

"Oh great," he groaned. "I'm going to be in trouble now. If you heard my father yesterday, you know I'm not supposed to have relationships with the natives."

"I'm not a native," Amy said.

"Well, you're a *human*, aren't you?"

That was an interesting question, but this was not the time or place to discuss the humanity of genetically designed clones. "And we're not having a relationship," she added.

That brought a brief smile to Meno's face. "Not *yet*."

These aliens were certainly pushy, Amy thought. "I just want my metal box. I think one of your people took it."

Meno looked apologetic. "They do things like that. It's a way of understanding the native population."

"But it's also stealing," Amy pointed out. "It's their land, Meno. They're entitled to have their own things. And they're not asking to be understood. Now just find my box and I'll leave before you get into any trouble."

"Follow me. I think I know where it could be." Meno led her out of the transport room. He checked the hallway to make sure no one was about and then hustled Amy into an empty elevator. It rose swiftly and opened onto another hallway. Placing a finger to his lips, Meno took Amy's hand and hurried her down the hall and into a room.

"This is where they keep the items taken from the natives. My father says it will all be in a museum someday." Amy saw shelves filled with stone tools, scraped pelts, and a necklace made of animal teeth on a leather thong. She wondered if it was Lulu's and if she could steal it back.

Then she saw her box. "That's it," she said, taking it off the shelf. She opened it to see if the patches were still inside.

Meno glanced nervously at the door, but he was also curious. "What is all that for?"

Amy showed him how the backing came off the patch. He took it and examined it.

"A person wears it on his arm," Amy explained. "Then, twenty-four hours later—"

At that instant they both heard footsteps outside the door. Meno grabbed Amy's hand and pulled her into a closet.

It was a tight fit. They huddled close together while whoever came in the room got what he or she wanted. When the door closed, Meno and Amy came out.

"I have to get you off this ship fast," Meno said. "Someone else could come."

Amy knew if that happened, Meno would be in more trouble than she would. All they could do to her was throw her off the ship. It was too bad she couldn't ask Meno to show her around. How many opportunities would she have to tour a spaceship? But she didn't want to see him get grounded by his father, or whatever alien parents did to their disobedient offspring. Tucking the metal box under her arm, she said, "Okay, let's go."

But when Meno reached out to take her hand, she didn't offer hers.

"What's wrong?" Meno asked.

"Meno—what's that on your hand?"

He looked to see what she was talking about. Rosy red bumps practically covered his palm, and the rash was moving up his arm. He was still holding the patch he'd taken from her. He hadn't even needed to wear it for twenty-four hours.

Poor Meno was completely dumbstruck. He had no idea what the rash was. Amy did.

"Ohmigod, Meno. You're the carrier. You brought the Plague to Earth."

twelve

Meno stared at the little red bumps. "I don't understand."

"It must be in your genes," Amy whispered.

"Am I sick?" he asked.

"No. It's probably perfectly normal for you to have the bacteria." After a pause, Amy said, "But it's killing humanity. Don't you see, Meno? This is the Plague that's going to kill people in the future!" Even as she said the words, looking at his sweet, stricken face, she couldn't see him as her mother's killer. But in a way, that was what he was.

As comprehension sank in, the horror on Meno's

face distorted his features. He flopped into a chair. Amy knelt next to him.

"But it's not too late, Meno! There's been no contact between your people and the Neanderthals. Your genes haven't mingled with theirs yet. If you can stop the colonization, the Plague won't happen!"

The color started to come back to his face. "You're right. If I tell the high council about the Plague, surely they'll see how wrong it is to take over this planet." He rose. "We'll go to my father."

This time, he made no effort to hide Amy as he led her to the office where his father would be. She received a number of odd glances from the humanlike aliens she passed on the way. They knew she was not one of them.

As did Meno's father. He looked up with a smile when Meno opened the door. The smile disappeared when he saw Amy behind his son.

He rose. "Meno! I told you, it is strictly forbidden to make contact with the natives! Why have you disobeyed me?"

"Father, she is not a native. She's a human from the future! You must hear her story."

But now Meno's father appeared even more distressed. "You are in grave danger, young woman. Quickly, we must send you back to Earth."

"No!" Amy cried out. "My mother's life is at stake! What you're doing here could mean the end of my civilization! You must listen to me." She poured out the story of the Plague, how it was believed to come from a genetic mutation in primitive mankind. She told him how she'd come back in time to search for an antidote, how Meno had reacted to the test patch. And before the man could stop her, she had ripped the backing off another patch and stuck it on his arm too.

"Look!" she cried out. She'd barely finished pressing the patch down before the pink-red rash began running up his arm. Aghast, he watched its progress.

"Do you see, Father?" Meno asked. "It is unethical for us to take over their world. If we do, we will destroy them. Not now, but sometime in the future."

Meno's father was grim. "We will go immediately to the high council."

The high council had already been warned of a human being's presence on their spaceship. When Amy, Meno, and Meno's father arrived at the council chambers, two men and a woman awaited them at a long table. On either side of the table stood two guards, holding metallic rods Amy suspected were weapons. Even in the tense atmosphere, she tried to absorb every detail. She was going to have amazing stories to tell when she got home.

If she got home. Meno's father presented her story to the council. Impassive, the trio listened.

They were not moved. "It is unfortunate that the human race will suffer in the future," one council member said. "However, our own civilization needs this planet, and we are a superior race. The colonization will continue as planned."

Amy turned to Meno's father. "No, you can't let this happen! Please!"

"Her mother could die!" Meno cried out.

But his father stepped back. "The council has spoken."

Amy couldn't believe what she was hearing. "Then I have to go back to the future and tell my people that I couldn't stop the Plague?"

The councilwoman spoke. "No, you will not go back to the future. If your people have time-travel technology, we cannot risk the possibility that they will come back to our time with an army to stop us."

Amy was in shock. "You mean you'll keep me here?"

"No," the woman said. "You will be eliminated."

"Excuse me?" Amy asked faintly.

"Your presence disrupts our plans." The woman nodded toward one of the guards, and he lifted his rod.

"No!" Meno cried out.

It was all happening too fast. Amy couldn't move.

Her entire life—and it wasn't very long—flashed before her eyes in the time it took the guard to activate his weapon. A white light shot out toward her and then was instantly gone.

Bewildered, Amy couldn't grasp what had just happened. She was still alive. Then a weight in her arms started to feel heavy. It was Meno.

Meno had rushed in front of her and blocked the white light. Instead of piercing Amy, it had pierced him. And he had collapsed in Amy's arms. A green liquid oozed from him. Then his whole body was transformed. His face became rounder, and his features flattened. His eyes darkened; his nose was reduced to something small and buttonlike. He wasn't horrible or monstrous. He was just Meno. And he was completely still.

Death had revealed his true face.

thirteen

There was chaos in the council chamber. Meno's father let out an unearthly wail. The council members rushed to Meno, while the guards reloaded their weapons. Meno's body was snatched from Amy's arms, and someone grabbed the metal box from her. The patches flew out, landing on the council members and the guards. Shouts and cries rang out as rosy rashes began to appear, even with the backings still on the patches. In the commotion, Amy fled.

They tried to stop her. A council member pursued her, and a guard shot a beam of light toward her, but this time she was prepared, and she ducked. She was faster than the alien giving chase, and she knew she could fight off any others who tried to stop her. But she had no idea where she was going.

The transport room. It had to be nearby. If she could find it, she could probably figure out how to get herself back to Earth. Ducking into an elevator, she went down to what she thought was the level she'd come in on. But as she raced in that direction, she heard an ominous sound in the distance. It sounded like a large group moving toward her. Guards? An army? Amy darted into the closest doorway.

She recognized the room she'd entered and realized she wasn't on the transport level. This was one flight up, the supply room where Meno had taken her to look for the metal box. She spotted Lulu's tooth necklace on a shelf.

Quickly, Amy stepped into the closet where she had hidden with Meno. She had to get back to Earth! She had to warn Lulu and the others about the aliens and their intentions. But what good would it do? The natives couldn't fight them, not with spears and harpoons. The aliens' technology was far superior.

Suddenly an enormous longing for home filled her. Home and humans, and one human in particular—her mother. If her mother was even living . . .

Could Amy signal Singularity? Was there a way to let

Sarah and Howard know they had to bring her back immediately?

The button they'd fixed to her clothes! That was the way!

And then she remembered that she had changed clothes after her bath. At this moment, the button was fixed to the dirty T-shirt that lay on the banks of the lake, along with her jeans and her backpack. Her one contact with Earth, and she'd left it behind. She just prayed that, unlike the wristwatch she'd once left by the sink in a public rest room and the hat she'd left on a playground, the button wasn't gone forever.

Her desire to get back to Stone Age Earth was stronger than ever. She pressed her ear against the closet door. There was no sound. So she pushed the door open.

Amy half expected to find a guard waiting, or Meno's father, who would surely be ready to kill her for causing the death of his son. But the room was still empty.

She crept out of the closet silently and started toward the door to the hall. Then she caught another glimpse of Lulu's tooth necklace. And even with all the anxiety and fear that surrounded her, she couldn't resist taking it, so she could bring it back to her friend.

It was a mistake. In the five seconds it took her to

lift the necklace and throw it around her neck, she had been located. The door to the room opened, and Meno's father stood before her.

She froze. Their eyes met. But there was no anger, no hatred in his look. Only immense sadness. He must have seen the same look in her eyes, because he nodded. Then he came forward and put a hand on her shoulder.

She thought she could pull away and free herself. He didn't seem to be armed, and her strength would probably be enough to shake him off. But for some reason, she didn't. Instead, she allowed him to bring her down the hall to the transport room.

A guard stood on duty outside the door. He raised his weapon. Meno's father put up a hand to stop him.

"Allow me to eliminate her," he said to the guard. "To avenge my son." The guard held the weapon out to him, and he took it. Still, Amy didn't try to get away. She wasn't even frightened. It was as if she sensed something in the man's gentle grip.

She wasn't wrong. In the next second, the door to the transport room opened. She was shoved in, the door was closed, and she found herself in a beam of light. It wasn't from a weapon. It was from the elevator-like light, and she felt herself moving down.

Once she was back on solid earth again, Amy looked

back up at the spaceship. It hovered, solid and unmoving, and she had no idea what was going on inside. With any luck, Meno's father would be unharmed. He might even be able to convince the council to discontinue colonization. Maybe she'd go back to her own time and find that the Plague had never even begun.

On the other hand, Meno's father could have been overpowered, and the aliens could be coming after her. She looked around to see if by any chance a dino taxi was in the area, but no such luck. She'd have to get back to the tribe on her own.

Moving swiftly, Amy headed beyond the woods, through the valley, and then over the ridge. She ran against the wind—maybe that was why her eyes were stinging. Or maybe it was because she was thinking about Meno, who had sacrificed himself to save her. No, not just her. He had sacrificed himself to save Earth. His father had tried too. Had they succeeded? She just hoped she'd be able to find out.

As she got within a few miles of camp, Amy could make out the figure of Lulu in the distance. The girl wasn't alone. There was a boy with her. The one she'd seen fishing? No, this boy wasn't in a fur. He wore jeans.

She gasped. "Andy. Andy!"

He saw her coming, and waved. But it wasn't a wave

of greeting. There was urgency in his gesture. Now she could hear him. "Quick, Amy, hurry! We have to go, my button is beeping!"

Amy shifted gears. She didn't think she had ever run this fast before in her life. But she'd never seen Andy so frantic, so worried.

She could also see that Lulu was utterly bewildered. Amy had to warn the cavegirl, to let her know what the aliens intended to do. But would she be able to make Lulu understand?

She wouldn't find out. Andy rushed forward to meet her. "I can feel it, they're pulling us back. Touch your button!"

"I'm not wearing it!" she shrieked.

Andy took a flying leap at her. Just as his arms wrapped around her, she felt the earth move. Somewhere, from far away, she heard Lulu's voice crying out, "My necklace!"

But there was no time for Amy to give it back. The world began to spin as she and Andy were sucked into the vortex of time.

fourteen

S arah and Howard looked very pleased with themselves. "Excellent," Sarah said as Amy and Andy emerged from the container. "You're alive and together."

"But we weren't together," Amy told them. "We didn't end up in the same place." She turned to Andy. "Where *were* you, anyway?"

"Looking for you!" Andy replied in an aggrieved tone. "I must have walked a hundred miles! And when I finally reached that community, everyone acted like I was going to mug them or something!"

"They thought you were one of the aliens," Amy murmured.

Howard and Sarah were suddenly alert. "Aliens!" Howard exclaimed. "There were aliens?"

"Aliens weren't on the scene for another millennium!" Sarah added. "Amy, you must tell us everything you saw."

"Not now," Amy said. "I have to go see my mother."

Andy was looking at her doubtfully. "You're going to the hospital dressed like that?"

Amy realized she was still in her cavegirl attire. On the one hand, this was Los Angeles—people would think she was wearing the latest style. On the other hand, her mother would kill her for going out like this. On the third hand—if her mother was capable of yelling, Amy wouldn't care about anything else.

But her mother wasn't capable of killing or yelling or anything of the sort. According to Dr. Dave, there had been no change.

Nancy Candler lay in the hospital bed, still and pale. "Can't you do something?" Amy pleaded.

Dr. Dave was just as distressed. But he was helpless. "This disease is a mystery, Amy. We don't know what to do for it."

"I know something about the Plague," Amy said. "It comes from aliens who visited Earth a quarter of a mil-

lion years ago. They infected the human population."
She didn't add that Meno's father hadn't been able to
stop them.

It wouldn't have mattered if she had. Dr. Dave was
now looking at her with serious concern. "Amy, are
you feeling all right?"

"I'm fine. I'm telling you, there were aliens. I was
there, I saw them. I tried to stop them, but . . ." And she
knew it was hopeless. Dr. Dave had to think she'd gone
completely insane.

"Amy," he said carefully, "I want you to sit down. I'm
going to call someone to talk to you."

But there was only one person Amy wanted to talk
to. One person who just might believe her—and who
could make a difference.

Andy was waiting for her in the hall outside her
mother's room. "Where are you going?" he asked as
she rushed out.

"I have to contact Mr. Devon."

"Amy, no!" He ran after her. Thank goodness there
was a phone booth with an old-fashioned door that she
could hold shut with her foot. While Andy pounded on
the glass, instant recall brought back the phone number that had appeared on her cell phone. She left a message. Then she walked out of the booth.

Andy had disappeared. She worried that he might be getting a psychiatrist to help him out. All she could hope was that Mr. Devon would show up before Andy returned.

He did. Amy got right to the point as soon as he appeared in the reception area. "I know where the genetic mutation came from. There were aliens." She told him the same story she'd told Dr. Dave. The difference was that Mr. Devon believed her.

"I want to give bone marrow," she said. "I'll do anything to save my mother."

"No!" It was Andy, coming rapidly toward them. Amy was relieved to see that he wasn't accompanied by men in white coats with a straitjacket. Even so, Andy could be dangerous.

"Andy, keep out of this," she said.

Andy spoke directly to Mr. Devon. "Don't take her bone marrow. Take mine."

"Andy!" Amy yelled.

Andy ignored her. "It wouldn't make any difference, right? My genes are as perfect as hers. Use me."

Mr. Devon's eyes darted back and forth between them. But they settled on Amy.

"What are you wearing?"

The question was unexpected. "What are you, the fashion police?" Amy quipped.

"It's a leopard skin," Andy supplied. "She got it from one of the Stone Age girls."

But it wasn't the fur that concerned Devon. "That dark green stain on the front," he said. "What is it?"

Amy looked down and winced. It was too easy to remember the green liquid oozing from Meno's body. "Blood, I guess. From an alien."

Slowly, Mr. Devon nodded. And then a hint of a smile spread across his face.

"Amy . . . I think you may have brought something back that's more valuable than bone marrow."

fifteen

Sitting on the edge of Nancy Candler's bed, Amy pushed a damp lock of hair off her mother's forehead. Nancy smiled weakly.

"I must look terrible."

"You look pretty good to me," Amy said. "What does Dr. Dave say?"

"He thinks I'll be able to go home in a few days. But he doesn't know why. No one has ever recovered from the Plague so quickly and so completely. He said every one of my tests is coming back normal."

Amy wished she could tell her that all the victims of the Plague would be recovering now. But this wasn't the right time. Nancy was too weak yet to hear Amy's strange story. She'd save it for the welcome-home party.

"What's that around your neck?" Nancy asked.

Amy fingered one of the teeth. "A horse-tooth necklace. Isn't it pretty?"

Her mother's eyes widened. "Sweetie, I don't know if that's such a nice thing. People shouldn't be making jewelry out of animal parts. That's as bad as wearing fur."

This wasn't the time for a mother-daughter argument either. Amy slipped the necklace off. "I'll be back soon," she promised, and kissed her mother's cheek.

Out in the hallway, Tasha, Eric, and Andy were waiting. "Those overalls look better on you than they do on me," Tasha said.

Amy grinned. "Thanks for bringing me some clothes."

"I wouldn't let you walk around naked after Mr. Devon took your leopard skin," Tasha assured her.

"I wouldn't mind," Eric murmured.

Andy made a mock fist and shook it in Eric's face. Then he looked at Amy and sighed. "Geez, it's not fair," he said. "Amy gets to do all the good stuff. She hangs with cave people, she goes inside a spaceship . . . and she saves the world."

Amy tried to be modest. "It was Meno who saved the

world. It was his blood on my clothes. Mr. Devon was able to take it for a DNA scan. That's how he came up with an antidote for my mother." Her brow wrinkled. "It's weird, though. How come he's acting like it's a secret? My mother doesn't know what cured her, and she said Dr. Dave doesn't know either."

"Devon's going to have to tell him eventually," Andy said. "Someone has to mass-produce this antidote."

"And come up with a vaccine so no one will get the Plague in the future," Tasha added. "Amy . . . did you really see dinosaurs?"

"That's impossible," Eric said. "There were no dinosaurs in the Stone Age."

"Textbooks aren't always right," Amy informed him.

Andy was still looking envious. "Now you can tell off the entire educational system. Man, you have all the luck."

Amy had to laugh. "Right. I'm going to tell the teachers of America that I went back to the Stone Age and saw dinosaurs. Like they're really going to believe me."

"Here comes Devon," Andy said.

The mystery man was coming toward them. Amy tried to read Andy's expression. He still didn't seem to be Devon's biggest fan. But maybe a tiny seed of trust had been planted.

Devon, as usual, was expressionless. He carried a package wrapped in brown paper, which he handed to Amy.

"I thought you might want to have a travel souvenir," he said.

Amy tore it open. It was the leopard skin she'd been wearing. "Don't you still need it for the bloodstain?"

"We got all we could get," Devon told her.

"Enough to cure everyone?" Tasha asked. "And create a vaccine?"

"No."

Expressions changed. Andy immediately became suspicious. "Why not?"

"The blood was exposed to the elements for too long. Cells were too damaged. We were only able to isolate enough for the one dose, which was given to Amy's mother."

"Can't you replicate it?" Amy asked.

"No, the chemical makeup is fragile. It would be like making photocopies of photocopies. The result is too weak. It won't help anyone."

"But—but I wanted to save people," Amy cried out in dismay. "Are you saying people will continue to suffer from the Plague? That nothing was accomplished?"

"You saved your mother," Devon said. "That's definitely something. And we learned some bits and pieces. For example, we now know that your bone marrow won't provide us with any useful information."

Andy was scowling. "I don't believe you," he said to Devon. "Something's going on here. There's a reason for the Plague. I think you know what it is, and I think it benefits you and your organization to keep it going."

Devon eyed him evenly. "Someday you'll know the truth. Not now." With that, he walked away.

Everyone was silent. As Amy tried to blink away tears, Eric put an arm around her. Andy calmed down and tried to start a conversation.

"You left your clothes in the Stone Age, right?" he said. "I wonder what they'll make of that metal button on your T-shirt. Maybe they'll figure out how to travel into the future. I wouldn't mind seeing that cavegirl again. What was her name?"

"Lulu," Amy said. "I left my cell phone there too. And a toothbrush."

"Yikes," Eric commented. "You remember on *Star Trek* when they talked about the Prime Directive?"

"Oh yeah," Andy said. "They had to be really careful not to change anything in the past, or they'd come back to a completely different future. I mean, present."

Amy looked around. "Nothing seems different to

me. I guess we didn't have any impact." She supposed that was a good thing, at least in *Star Trek* terms. But it made her profoundly sad.

The others were chatting now, about what the cave people would do with cell phones and toothbrushes. Amy tried to join in, but her heart just wasn't with them. She knew she should be grateful. After all, she had saved her mother.

But she hadn't saved the world.

The Plague was still very much among them. . . .

Don't miss

replica

Play

The Plague Trilogy
Book II

This just in! Body counts from the plague keep mounting!

Amy's encounter with dinosaurs and cave dwellers—and aliens—was pretty wild. Now her quest to stop the spread of the infectious bacteria gets even more bizarre as she agrees to take another perilous voyage.

A voyage inside a plague-ridden human body.

If Amy survives being injected into this complex landscape where good cells are waging battle against bad cells, she could save millions of lives. But it's a do-or-die world in there. . . .